'I should have taken you for a phoney from the start. Why didn't you tell me the truth?'

'Would you have taken me on if you'd known who I was?'

'Of course not.'

'There's your answer, Jason. I detest lying—I never do it as a rule—but I knew you wouldn't consider me the moment I mentioned Todd's name.'

'In other words, you lie whenever you're unable to get your own way,' he said contemptuously.

Nicola fought back the tears that welled in her eyes.

ECHOES IN THE NIGHT

BY
ROSEMARY CARTER

MILLS & BOON PTY. LIMITED
SYDNEY · AUCKLAND · MANILA
LONDON · TORONTO

Published by
Mills & Boon Pty. Limited
72-74 Gibbes Street
Chatswood, NSW 2067
Australia

First published in Great Britain 1990
Australian copyright 1990
New Zealand copyright 1990
Philippine copyright 1990
First Australian paperback edition August 1990
© Rosemary Carter 1990

ISBN 0 263 76708 6

Printed in Australia by
The Book Printer,
Victoria

CHAPTER ONE

'Not even a hello? How's that for a welcome?'

'Nicola. . .' Todd Armstrong looked up from his book. 'I'm sorry, sis, I didn't hear you come in.'

'I know you didn't. When you're working on your book, the sound of a mere door is the last thing to register.' Nicola was laughing, but gently, for she knew the strain her half-brother had been under in the months since the accident.

Todd took off his glasses and rubbed eyes that were a little like Nicola's, eyes they had both inherited from their mother.

'You're right,' he said apologetically. 'I was far away, in the veld somewhere. In the mountains. . . Anywhere but in an apartment in Cape Town.'

'I'll bet you haven't eaten today.'

He glanced at a plate which held the remains of a doughnut. Beside it was a can of beer which had gone flat hours ago. 'Not very much,' he admitted.

'Just as well I brought you some good things, then. Smoked snoek, salad, a French loaf. And some wine to make it all taste better.'

There had always been a close bond between them. Todd had been a little boy when his father had died and his mother had married John Malloy. Nicola was the product of that second marriage. As a child, she had been Todd's shadow, a pretty little girl who adored her brother and was never happier than when she was allowed to play with him and his friends.

The little girl had grown into a beautiful young

woman, Todd decided, as he watched her lay out the food. Her smooth shoulder-length hair was the colour of polished mahogany, her eyes were a deep, sparkling brown, and her lips curved in a way which, he knew, many men found irresistible. What amazed him was that Nicola, at the age of twenty-two, had never been more than fleetingly attracted to any of them.

Nicola straightened the apartment while Todd ate. There were papers everywhere, and she knew better than to touch them. Her brother knew his way around his muddle. It was when books were put on shelves and papers were ordered that he became frantic. The kitchen and bedroom were another matter. Nicola hated dirt, and she washed dishes and dusted grimy surfaces and generally made the apartment habitable.

When she had finished, she pulled up a chair beside Todd. 'How was the meal?' she asked.

'Delicious. You brought some good things, Nicola.'

'Food isn't all I brought.'

'Sounds interesting.'

Nicola took a newspaper from her tote-bag. 'Seen this yet?'

'I was going to go out and get one a bit later.'

'There's an article that might interest you.'

Something in her voice caught him. 'Oh?'

She opened the paper and put it in front of him. 'There,' she said, and gestured.

It did not take him long to read the short piece. When he had finished, he looked back at her, and she saw that his eyes were troubled. 'Another tour to the Drakensberg.'

'The same route as the last one?'

'Same route, different group leader.'

'Did you know?'

'No reason why they'd have told me. There's absolutely no chance that Jason would take me on again,' he said grimly.

'You can't be sure of that.'

'My days with Adventure Tours are over. With any other tour group as well. Face it, Nicola, after the bad publicity I received in some of the Cape Press, if I haven't been blacklisted already, I will be.'

'You did nothing wrong, Todd,' she assured him.

'*I* know that. And for some reason you believe me. You're the only one who does.'

'I know you didn't move the sign warning that the bridge was unsafe.'

'I didn't even *see* the darn thing. That's what bothers me. I don't know how I could have missed it—both Jason and Lance swear it was there. The fact is, I *did* miss it. Sometimes I think——' Todd stopped.

'It's not as if anything disastrous happened. You lost your spools with all your photos, and the other two men damaged their cameras. And you all got a bit wet in the stream, of course. But there were no major injuries.'

'Three of us were stranded on the wrong side of a broken bridge while the rest had to go back for help. By the time they got back to the camp it was already dusk. Jason had to organise a rescue expedition with torches and a stock of emergency rations.'

'I still say nothing major happened,' Nicola insisted.

'My credibility was destroyed. And with it my chances of becoming a botany lecturer.'

'You don't know that.'

'I'm pretty certain.'

'But, Todd, that's so unfair!' she protested.

'Pretend you're a stranger, Nicola. How does it look to you? And try to see it with an unprejudiced eye for once, if you can. Todd Armstrong gets himself a job with Adventure Tours, not only to earn some extra money for his research, but also to further it. The tour company just happens to take people to the very place where Todd wants to be. While on the job, he has a chance to take photographs.'

'Please stop,' Nicola pleaded. 'I can't bear to see you so upset.'

'There is one special plant,' her half-brother went on relentlessly. 'An unusual aloe, unique, and almost inaccessible. A flower which he mentions in his book as being known to exist. If he manages to find it, to photograph it, the photo will be the highlight of the book. The aloe is so important to him that he's prepared to risk the safety of the group he's leading, just to take a picture of it.'

'That's ridiculous,' Nicola protested. 'If the aloe was really so important, you could have gone on your own, in your own time. You didn't need the tour.'

'But I did. It's a tough trip to do alone. You really do need other people. Camps and horses and a good stock of food—resources which I could never afford.'

'Maybe——' she began.

Todd folded the newspaper. 'Thanks for bringing this. I know you meant well. Unfortunately, I can't do anything with it.'

'But I can.'

She smiled as Todd stared at her and said, 'You're crazy, Nicola!'

'Not in the least.'

'What's on your mind?' he asked.

'I'm going on the tour,' Nicola told him.

'No, Nicola!'

'I'll bring back the pictures you need.'

'You don't even know that you could find the purple

aloe.' He grimaced as he saw her smile. 'Don't make anything of that—the idea's out of the question.'

'I might not find *the* aloe,' her eyes were sparkling now, 'but I could take other photos. Replace the ones you lost when your spools dropped in the stream.'

'Nicola. . .'

'And I could try to find out what really happened at the bridge.'

'You don't know how you're tempting me,' said Todd with a groan.

'Good. Because I just happen to have a few weeks' leave from the modelling studio, and I mean to spend it in the mountains. I'm a dab hand with a camera, and you've taught me a fair bit about flowers.'

'You're breaking down all my defences,' he said weakly.

'You don't have any defences, Todd.'

'I do have one. You're my sister. Jason Langley would never consider taking you on the tour.'

'*Half*-sister,' she reminded him. 'Your name is Armstrong, mine is Malloy.'

'True. . .'

'Besides which, I don't see why I should have anything to do with Jason. You told me he accompanies a different tour every time. He went to the Drakensberg the last trip, so he won't go that way again for a while.

'You've really thought this thing out, Nicola,' Todd admitted ruefully.

'Yes, I have.'

'I don't know what to say.'

'Just say yes, idiot! You've done so much work on the book, Todd. You don't want to see it all go for nothing just because of an accident that wasn't your fault.'

'It's like a miracle,' Todd said slowly. 'Just when I'd

given up all hope, you come along with this idea. I don't know how to thank you.'

'You can treat me to a slap-up champagne dinner when I get back,' Nicola said lightly. 'I'll apply tomorrow.'

'I hope you manage to get on to the tour. It's the last one before winter. There'll be nothing for months after this.'

'I'll get on to it,' she promised.

Adventure Tours had spacious premises in the heart of the city. The walls were lined with attractive posters advertising the various expeditions. There was a trip for people interested in the wilder places along the Garden Route, and one that explored the ancient mysteries of the Kalahari Desert. A bushman painting, blown up and a little exaggerated, advertised the Drakensberg trip which Todd Armstrong had once helped to lead.

But when Nicola sat down with a travel consultant, she was given disappointing information. 'That tour is booked up, Miss Malloy.'

'It can't be! I read about it only yesterday.'

'It's one of our most popular tours, and it was first advertised weeks ago,' the consultant said apologetically. 'The last remaining spaces were taken up yesterday, after the article appeared in the paper.'

'I so badly want to go along,' Nicola said.

'There'll be another tour in a few months. Why don't I put you down for that?'

'I want to go this time.'

'I wish I could help you. . . .'

'I wish it too. But. . .'

Nicola's words trailed away as a man walked into the agency. A tall man, rugged and broad-shouldered, with a look of the wild outdoors despite the expensive suit that clothed his body. As he passed the consultant's desk, grey eyes, the colour of steel, briefly touched Nicola's face.

'Morning, Carol,' he said, before walking into an office and closing the door behind him.

'That man. . . Does he work here?' asked Nicola.

'He's Mr Langley. He owns Adventure Tours.'

'*Jason* Langley?'

'Yes. Why?'

Nicola stood up. 'I have to talk to him.'

'You can't do that,' Carol protested, but Nicola, to whom the trip had become a mission, was already walking away from the consultant's desk.

She knocked on the closed door. At the quiet 'Come in' she went inside.

Jason Langley was standing by the window. He had taken off his jacket and was loosening his tie. As he turned and saw Nicola, his eyebrows lifted in surprise.

'Don't blame Carol,' Nicola said quickly, before he could speak. 'She tried to stop me coming in here.'

'I'm sure she did. Who are you? And are you in the habit of forcing yourself on to people?' He looked her over coolly.

Nicola felt herself go warm under the look. 'I can understand that you're angry, Mr Langley. But I had to see you.'

Another cool look out of a face that was disturbingly exciting. It was a face of hard lines, of high cheekbones, and a taut tanned skin, of lips that were both sensuous and strong.

'I want to go on your Drakensberg tour,' said Nicola, a little unsteadily.

'Carol is the person to talk to.'

'She says the tour is full.'

'There'll be others—she must have told you that.'

'I want to go on this one, Mr Langley.'

'We can take only so many people. The best we can do is put you on the waiting-list.'

'I've set my heart on this trip,' she insisted.

His eyes were on her, assessing her. 'Suppose you tell me why?'

'I'm very interested in wild shrubs and flowers. Especially the ones found in the mountains.'

'That still doesn't explain why it has to be this particular trip. Are you a student? Or a writer? Do you have a deadline of some sort?'

Nicola was inherently an honest person. She avoided lies, believing the truth was better in most circumstances. But this was an unusual situation.

'I'm a photographic model,' she told him. 'I have to fit in my leave with my assignments, and I don't know when my spare time will coincide with another one of your trips.'

He was silent for at least a minute. The eyes that searched her face seemed to hold a question. Nicola sat quite still, making an effort not to betray her tension as she waited for him to speak.

Suddenly he smiled. In a moment he was transformed. Warmth chased the coolness from his face, and around his eyes and mouth were the lines of a person who loved life and laughter. By any standard, Jason Langley was an attractive man. The combination of warmth with all that tough, sexy strength made him dynamic.

'I don't know your name,' he said.

'Nicola Malloy.'

'Strange,' he said thoughtfully. 'I don't know anyone by that name, and yet there's something about you that's familiar. Something in the eyes. . .'

So that was the reason for the question she'd glimpsed

in his face. He had picked up the resemblance to Todd. Nicola felt herself tense.

With a lightness she was far from feeling, she said, 'I don't believe we've ever met.'

'If we had, I would have remembered,' he said drily. 'It will come to me, I suppose.' He picked up a pen. 'Look, Miss Malloy, the tour is full, that happens to be a fact. There are only so many seats in our vehicles and each one is taken up. I'm sorry, but that's the way it is.'

She was walking to the door when his next words stopped her. 'There is just one other possibility.'

'*Oh?*' she queried.

'Though I don't imagine you'd be interested.'

'Try me,' she said eagerly.

'There's a vacancy on our staff.'

'I'll take it.'

He laughed, a low, vibrant laugh that was as attractive as the rest of him. 'You don't even know what it is yet! We need a cook, Miss Malloy.'

'I can cook,' she assured him.

'You're a photographic model.'

'I once spent a summer holiday helping as a cook at a youth camp. And I know my way around a kitchen.'

'Normally we expect references,' he went on. 'With thirty people on the tour, we have to be certain that the meals are good.'

The grey eyes were teasing, but Nicola understood that the words had not been idly spoken. She met Jason Langley's look with a dancing one of her own. 'Unfortunately I can't give you anything in writing. But I do have an idea. Let me cook you a meal, Mr Langley. You could make up your mind after that.'

'Done.' He looked unexpectedly pleased. 'Tonight?'

Just as well that she and Todd did not share a home. 'I'll give you my address,' she said.

'No,' said Jason Langley. 'We'll have the meal at my apartment.'

'But that way I can't prepare anything in advance.'

'Exactly.'

'I don't understand.'

'I want to know that whatever you serve was made without help. I'll buy the supplies, you'll do the cooking.' He scribbled a few words on a piece of paper, then held it out to her. 'My address. I'll be expecting you at seven, Miss Malloy.'

Jason Langley opened the door at Nicola's first knock. For a long moment he stood quite still, and there was the oddest look in his eyes, almost as if he was surprised for some reason. But he recovered himself quickly.

'Hello, Miss Malloy,' he said easily, smiling as he stepped aside to let her in.

On the way over Nicola had tried telling herself that he was not really all that attractive. But she knew the moment she saw him again that she had been mistaken. Jason Langley was the most attractive man she had ever met.

She looked past him, into a room that seemed all light and space and huge glass windows, and forced herself to make conversation.

'What a wonderful place!'

'Glad you like it.'

She walked to a spot where two windows met in an angle. 'You must be able to see the whole of Cape Town from here.'

'A large part of it,' he agreed.

He had come up behind her. She did not have to turn to see his smile—she could hear it in his voice.

She moved her eyes to take in a different view. 'And from this window you could think you were on a ship.'

'There've been many times when I let myself think that.'

He was standing beside her now. Though he was not crowding her, she was intensely aware of his physical presence. He was invading her private space in a way that made her feel excited and a little nervous.

So she went on making conversation. 'The ocean looks so peaceful. Seeing it like this, you'd never guess how wild the Atlantic can be sometimes.'

'You'll have to see my view one day when there's a storm. I think you'll be impressed, Nicola.'

The unexpected use of her first name made something leap inside her. 'Since I'm only here to pass a one-time test, it's unlikely that I'll ever do that,' she said briskly. And before he could reply to that, 'Well now, I should start cooking.'

'No hurry,' he said lazily.

She turned to look at him at that. He was smiling down at her, bringing a most unusual kind of gentleness to a face that was more rugged than any she knew.

'It's why I'm here,' she said, not quite steadily.

'I haven't forgotten. Nor have I invited you for anything else. No ulterior motives, if that's what you're thinking, Nicola.'

'I would hope not!' She was all briskness again.

'You have my assurance. I thought we'd sit on the patio a while, enjoy the view and the sunset. Get ourselves in the right mood for our meal.'

The patio jutted beyond the outer wall of the penthouse apartment. Far below, the waves crashed on to the rocks, and the sound of the ocean was a constant thunder. If you looked to the right you saw Table Mountain and the city that crowded its lower slopes. If you looked straight ahead, all you saw was water.

Nicola sat back on her white cane chair, and watched Jason Langley mix them each a shandy.

'Thanks,' she said, as she took the glass from him.

'Cheers.' He sat down in the chair beside her, and lifted his glass towards hers. 'To a pleasant trip.'

'Isn't this toast a bit premature? I haven't passed the test yet.'

'You've passed part of it already.'

'Which part?' she asked.

'You don't really want an evaluation at this stage, do you?' His eyes sparkled.

A note of caution sounded in her mind. She was getting on far too well with this man she would not see again, no matter how pleasantly they passed the evening together.

'I may not pass the rest of the test—the important part.'

'I have confidence in you, Nicola. You have the look of a girl who can cope with life.'

'Is that the impression I give? There was a time when women liked men to think of them as frail and helpless.'

'Just as well I didn't live then, because I would never have found myself attracted to any of them,' he said softly.

It was time to get back to the topic in hand. 'I assume you have all the ingredients I'll need?' asked Nicola.

'Every one. But let's not talk about food till we've finished our sundowners.'

Nicola watched as Jason Langley took a sip of his shandy. The hand that held the glass was big and tanned and well shaped, and it occurred to her how exciting it would be to feel his hands caressing her body. A moment later she had pushed the thought forcefully from her mind.

Instead she looked again at the view. 'I can see why

you wouldn't want to waste this wonderful sunset with a meal.'

'In the wild my habits change,' he explained. 'But when I'm on civilised terrain, with all the luxuries of electricity, I enjoy eating when it's dark.'

Nicola laughed. 'I think I can understand that. In the bush you'd have to get your meal—or at least the bulk of the preparation—done before sunset.'

'I've been waiting for you to relax long enough to laugh,' Jason Langley said.

Nicola swung around. She was always so at ease with men, but this one had a way of making her feel strangely young and unsure of herself.

'I'm not sure what you mean by that,' she said slowly.

'Are you going to tell me why you've been looking so tense?'

'I didn't know I looked tense.'

'All the talk about the view—it never really meant anything did it?'

Nicola hesitated. She could hardly tell him that while his physical presence had struck a chord somewhere deep inside her own body, her mind was concerned with the problem of how he would react if he knew she was Todd Armstrong's sister.

'I'm wondering whether I'll pass the rest of the test,' she said.

'That's all there is to it?'

'What else could there be?' she asked lightly.

'If I knew that, Nicola, I wouldn't be asking you.'

He was perceptive, this man. Thank the lord he would not be along on the trip! It would be too hard to keep secrets from him.

'I'd like to see you laugh again,' he said. 'I like a girl who laughs with her eyes as well as her teeth.'

That did get her laughing, and this time she could

actually feel the sparkle that lit her eyes. 'You'll turn my head with your compliments, Mr Langley.'

'You're too sensible to let that happen. And why are you calling me Mr Langley when I've been calling you Nicola?'

'You're the boss.'

'Which we haven't altogether established yet. All the more reason to call me Jason.'

'Jason. . .' she said.

They smiled at each other. It was a moment of almost perfect harmony. Falling in love would have to be a little like this, Nicola thought.

'Tell me about yourself,' he said then.

'There isn't much to tell.'

'You must love flowers very much to want to join the tour so badly.'

'I do. I've dreams of studying botany some day.' That was true, for thanks to Todd the subject had always fascinated her. 'How about you, Jason? What is your interest?'

He crossed one leg over another, and took a sip of his shandy before answering. He was wearing cords, and the moulded fabric hinted at thighs and calves that were taut and muscular. The shoulders and chest beneath a cotton-knit shirt had the same suggestion of strength and muscularity.

'I enjoy bushmen paintings and ancient artefacts, that kind of thing,' he said.

'Are you an anthropologist?'

'Not in the traditional sense of the word. It's my hobby, as botany is yours. Basically, I'm a businessman, Nicola. I operate a tour company for people who want to get to the wilder, more isolated parts of the country.'

'Who goes on the tours?' she asked.

'All sorts—teachers, scientists, writers, students.

Some just want to have fun, others are extremely serious about the things they want to see. We try to cater for them all.'

'I've heard'—she hesitated just for a moment—'that you yourself go on a different tour every time?'

'That's right. I never go to the same place twice in a row.'

So what Todd had said was true. Since Jason had been on the last Drakensberg tour, he would not be guiding the next one.

The sunset began to fade over the water, and it grew dark. Jason seemed quite content to continue sitting on the patio. But Nicola was suddenly restless.

'I think it's time to cook,' she said.

CHAPTER TWO

NICOLA followed Jason back into the penthouse, through the spacious living-room and into the kitchen.

She was not surprised to find that the kitchen was a dream. A long room, a blend of chrome and glass and gleaming copper, it was all any person who loved cooking could want. Jason opened the fridge and brought out a packet of steak. There were mushrooms in a brown paper bag, and vegetables and a mixture of salad ingredients. In the grocery cupboard were exotic packets and tins and interesting sauces, and on the counter was a rack with varied herbs and spices.

'If there's anything you need, say the word and I'll run out and get it,' said Jason.

'Actually, I'm amazed to find so much food in the kitchen of a bachelor-explorer.' She saw him grin. 'Or did you lay in all this stuff just for tonight?'

'Some of it,' he admitted, as he swung his long legs over a high bar stool.

Conscious that the test had begun, she said, 'Look, why don't you go and listen to music or something, and I'll call you when I'm ready?'

'I think I'll stay where I am.'

'You want to make sure that I'm efficient and orderly and that I don't sneak in some good take-out food.'

Grey eyes glinted. 'Maybe I just enjoy watching you.'

His presence was disturbing. But she wanted to pass the test, so she tried to push him from her mind as she planned her menu. Steak, of course, grilled in a delicate blending of sauces. A minute or two before it was ready, she would layer the top of the meat with chopped mushrooms. Wild rice would be good, as would carrots glazed in honey and a tossed salad.

Dessert was the problem. Nicola loved to cook, and she would have liked to make something so wickedly decadent that if Jason had any reservations left about taking her on, the wonder of her dessert would decide the outcome of the test. However, amply as the kitchen was stocked, she could find nothing with which to end the meal.

'Don't worry about dessert now,' said Jason. 'Time to think about that afterwards.'

A solarium led off from the kitchen, and that was where they ate. It was a lovely room, informal and cosy, with charcoal sketches of the Kruger National Park and the Garden Route covering the walls, and plants everywhere. Between two deep chairs there was an imbuia table on which Jason had set out woven mats, cutlery and elegantly shaped glasses.

Nicola was surprised to see candles and wine.

'This is supposed to be a test, Jason,' she said.

'I haven't forgotten. Do you have something against candles and wine?'

'I love them! But they add flavour and zest to any meal.'

'If they add to our enjoyment, why do you care?'

'It seems less of a test somehow,' she said.

He looked at her. 'Why do I get the feeling that's not really the problem?'

'The dinner is beginning to feel more like a date than a test.' She spoke a little too quickly.

The look he subjected her to was unsettling. 'You've cooked a delicious meal, Nicola. Why don't you just sit back and enjoy it?'

'If you say so.' She felt suddenly light-headed.

It would have been hard not to enjoy herself after that. Besides being the most attractive man Nicola had ever met, Jason was also the best company. In no time they were exchanging stories: his concerned people he'd encountered in the course of his travels, hers had to do with her more unusual modelling experiences.

They were halfway through the meal when he lifted his glass to her. 'To a wonderful trip.'

'You mean I've passed the test?'

'Didn't you know?'

'We haven't even had dessert yet!' she protested.

'I told you not to think about that.'

They went on talking, the easy conversation of two people who had always been friends. Only when Jason asked about her family did Nicola become wary.

'Mom and Dad died some time ago,' she said.

'You're alone in Cape Town, then?'

She hesitated just a moment. 'I do have a brother.'

'See much of him?'

'When he's in town,' she said, a little vaguely.

'What does he do?'

'Oh. . .research. . . A bit of this, a bit of that. How about you, Jason, do you have family?'

He told her about his parents, who were sheep-farmers, and about an eccentric bachelor uncle who had included him in his trips around the world. Jason was twenty when he was asked to lead a student group to the Kruger National Park. A few months later he had led another group of young people, this time on a climbing tour up Table Mountain.

'When the travelling bug bites, it bites hard,' he said. 'I was young, restless, and never happier than when I was on the move. I realised that I enjoyed being a leader and an organiser, and that I got a real thrill out of taking people to places they might not want to go to on their own.'

'That would be exciting!'

'The really exciting bit was understanding that I could turn my hobby into business. Of course, I don't do it all alone. I find people who are experts in their fields, and they become group leaders. Most of the time it works well. Though sometimes'—he frowned—'we run into problems.'

Nicola held her breath as she wondered if Jason was going to speak about Todd. But Jason did not mention him. Nor did he ask Nicola again about her brother. That dangerous moment had passed when she had managed to turn the subject back to himself.

They were still talking when they carried the dishes into the kitchen. Jason insisted on helping with the washing up, saying that this part of the meal was not included in the test.

'Time for dessert,' he said, when the kitchen was tidy.

'I'll need a few things for that, Jason.'

'All you need is your bag and your jacket.'

'I don't understand.'

'I'm taking you out for dessert, Nicola.' He met her surprised stare with an amused look of his own. 'I've been told there's a wonderful new place in town.'

Nicola had also heard of the new restaurant set high on the mountain slope, though she had never been there. The place was crowded. There was just one vacant table by the window, but Jason managed to get it, despite the disappointment of other prospective patrons. He was the kind of man who would usually get what he wanted, Nicola thought, and he would do it not with aggression but with his own kind of rugged charisma.

Over Nicola's half-hearted protests, Jason ordered for

them both a concoction that was made with Grand
Marnier, heavy cream and fat glacé cherries.

'I was going to make you something decadent, but
nothing quite like this,' she said. 'Lord, Jason, think of
the calories!'

'Forget the calories,' he laughed.

'Just for tonight,' she agreed.

'I don't know why a beautiful woman with a figure
like yours would need to think of calories at all.'

The flippant answer Nicola was about to give died on
her tongue as she saw the look he gave her. A look that
lingered on her lips a few seconds before moving over
the rest of her body. A male look that was so thoroughly
searching and seductive that she found herself trembling.

Deliberately she turned to the window, pretending an
intense interest in the lights of a distant ship. It was half
a minute at least before her trembling stilled, and she
was able to meet Jason't eyes once more.

The Grand Marnier dessert was light and wonderful.
When they had finished eating, Jason reached across the
table for Nicola's hand and said, 'I want to dance with
you.'

Wordlessly, she followed him on to the dance-floor.
People were doing modern steps to the music, which was
light and lively. But Jason held out his arms, and she
went into them. He did not hold her tightly, just close
enough for her cheek to rest against his shoulder. He
barely had to lead her, they moved together in the kind
of unison of couples who had been dancing together all
their lives.

After a while they went back to their table and the
waiter came and poured them more coffee. And when
they had only half finished drinking it, they returned to
the dance-floor.

This time Jason held her more closely. Nicola knew

she should insist on some space for herself, but there was a part of her that was beyond protest. Earlier his free hand had been on her back, but now both hands were on her waist. The tips of his fingers firmed on her hips, and in seconds her body turned to fire. She was conscious of every inch of the long body that moved against hers. She felt the beating of his heart against her throat, the hardness of his thighs against her stomach. His lips moved in her hair, and she had to stop herself from lifting her head for his kiss.

Closing her eyes, she let her body move with his. She went dancing often, but no dancing had ever been like this. Never before had she experienced a harmony that turned two bodies into one, a sensuousness that replaced all thought with sensation. There was just one thing in her mind, and that was the wish that the dance would never end.

It was only when the band stopped for a break, and they went back to their table, that Nicola remembered the reality of Jason's role in her brother's life, and in her own. Somehow, in the last few hours, she had let herself forget that fact. Tonight was not a date, even if it had all the makings of one.

'It's late,' she said, with a deliberate glance at her watch.

'We've hours left of the evening.'

'I do have to go.' She moved restlessly in her chair.

Jason looked at her through the candle-light, his eyes hooded now and difficult to read. 'Why, Nicola?'

'I think it's best.'

He did not press her to change her mind. They were both silent as he drove her home. It was a silence that was in strange contrast to their easy conversation earlier in the evening.

It was only when Jason stopped the car in front of her Sea Point apartment that Nicola turned to him.

'What happens now?' she asked.

'What would you like to happen?' he asked softly.

'Will I see you——?' She stopped, unable to believe the words that had almost escaped her, glad that it was too dark for him to see her flush. 'What I mean is. . . Will you be letting me know the details of the trip?'

'The tour organiser, Jane Broadbent, will get in touch with you in a day or two,' he said. 'She'll be able to tell you everything you need to know.'

'Yes. . . Well, that's good.' She felt totally deflated.

'I think you'll enjoy the trip, Nicola.'

'I know I will,' she said firmly. 'Well, Jason, I'd best be going. I'm really glad I passed the test. Thanks for a nice evening.'

'Thank you too,' he said, very politely.

With her hand on the car door she turned to him. 'Earlier. . .even before I started cooking. . .you said I'd already passed a portion of the test.'

'You had.'

'*How*?'

'You were so determined to go on the tour that you didn't mind signing on as camp cook. That had to get you an A-plus for resourcefulness.'

The next question came out almost without her thinking about it. 'Do you do lots of employee testing, then? At your home, I mean. . .'

'Tonight was the first time,' he told her.

'Oh!'

'It's the first time I've been invited to do such a test. And there's something else I've never done with an employee, Nicola.'

'What's that?'

'This,' he said, and reached for her.

Nicola's hand tightened on the door, then dropped as Jason's arms closed around her. His kiss was tender, lingering, demanding no response beyond anything she wanted to give. The feel of his lips was so sweet, so achingly seductive, that her own lips began to part beneath his.

It was at least a minute before the reality of what was happening struck her. Horrified, she moved her mouth from his.

'Nicola. . .?'

'Goodnight.' Her voice shook.

'Goodnight,' Jason said softly. As she opened the door of the car, he made no effort to detain her.

'Run that by me again,' said Todd, looking dazed.

'I'm leaving on the Drakensberg tour next week.'

'The other bit, Nicola.'

'You don't mean the bit about being the tour cook?' she teased.

'*That* bit.'

'The tour is fully booked, not a single vacancy. But it just so happens that the usual cook can't make it this time. It seemed the only solution.'

'Aren't you taking this thing very far beyond the bounds of sisterly devotion?' asked Todd.

'It was the only way I could get on to the tour. Don't look so upset, Todd. I don't mind. In fact, I think it might be rather fun cooking for a whole group of people.'

'You might curse yourself for taking it on.'

'I don't think so. Just think, Todd. . . It's not only the purple aloe, though I intend to find that. It's also the bridge. Wouldn't it be wonderful if I could find out what really happened that day?'

'It would be more than wonderful.'

'I'll do it,' Nicola promised. Then she said, 'Listen, Todd. . . There's something I haven't told you.'

'What's that?'

'I spent the evening with Jason Langley.'

'*You did what?*' he demanded.

'I was at his apartment.' Nicola took a look at her brother's shocked face, and went on quickly, 'I realised he wouldn't take me on unless he knew I could cope, so I offered to cook him a meal.'

'I don't believe it!'

'As a kind of test.'

'Did he give you a hard time?'

'A very pleasant time, actually.' Nicola paused. In a different voice, she said, 'Afterwards he took me out for dessert and dancing.'

'*Nicola!*'

'I didn't plan it that way, Todd,' she assured him.

'Does he know who you are?'

'No. Though I felt awkward not telling him, especially when he said something about my eyes being familiar.'

'Just as well you didn't,' Todd said grimly.

'I suppose so. . . Although he's not the ogre I thought he would be.'

'I never said Jason was an ogre. But he can get extremely angry—as I found out to my cost. You definitely don't want to be on the wrong side of him, Nicola.'

'Tell me about him, Todd,' she invited.

'He's built up quite a business, he's a great success in his field.'

'How old is he?'

'Thirty-three, thirty-four.'

'Is he married?'

Her brother shot her a suspicious glance. 'Why do you ask?'

'Just wondering,' she said lightly.

'He was married once, long ago. Apparently it didn't work out because his wife couldn't accept his kind of life.'

'And there's been nobody since?'

'If there has been I don't know about it.'

'Hm. . .' she said thoughtfully.

'*Nicola*!' Todd looked quite alarmed now. 'You didn't fall for him, did you?'

'He's rather dynamic, in case you hadn't noticed.'

'You're not the first woman to think that. The girls swarm around Jason Langley in droves. You should see them on tour sometimes! Heaven knows why they find him so irresistible.'

'Because he is irresistible,' Nicola said drily.

'Hell, I don't believe this! Only the other day I was wondering why no man is good enough for you. And here you are, falling for the one man who can never be for you!'

'I didn't say I'd fallen for him.'

'I hope not, sis. For one thing, imagine his reaction if he found out you were my sister. He'd think you'd tricked him.'

'He'd be right, because I have. But he won't find out, so don't look so worried, Todd.'

'I don't want you to break your heart over Jason.'

'That isn't likely to happen,' Nicola said reasonably. 'He *is* attractive. And if I'd met him in a different situation, then maybe. . . As it is, I can't imagine I'll ever see Jason Langley again. He went on the Drakensberg tour last time, he'll go on a different tour this time.'

'That's right,' Todd said slowly. 'It's the way he operates.'

'Then you really don't have any cause for concern. It's obvious that I won't see him again.'

Next day Nicola arranged a meeting with Jane Broadbent. A friendly, competent woman, Jane had been organising the staff side of Adventure Tours almost from its inception. In less than an hour she had explained the duties of a tour cook.

She told Nicola about the supplies which would be carried up the mountain on horseback, about the base camp where the bulk of the things would be kept, about the rations which would have to be carried in rucksacks in those areas where the horses could not go. She gave her a list of fresh and canned and dehydrated foods. In a folder was a set of suggested menus.

'Have I left anything out?' she asked at last.

Nicola smiled at her. 'I don't think so. You seem to have thought of everything.'

'And you do think you'll cope?'

'I hope so.'

It was Jane's turn to smile. 'You'll be fine. Jason spoke highly of you, and he's a good judge of character.'

Two days before the tour was due to leave, there was a meeting of all the staff. The meeting was held in the afternoon in the offices of Adventure Tours.

Carol, the consultant who had spoken to Nicola the first time, showed her where to go. Early as Nicola was, there were others already in the room; a few men and a tall curly-haired girl. They were all gathered around a coffee urn, chatting.

Nicola stood in the doorway, looking at them. No sign of Jason. Slowly she expelled a breath and forced herself to relax. Until that moment she had not dared acknowledge to herself quite how much she'd been hoping to see him again.

Just then the curly-haired girl turned, saw her, and came towards her with an outstretched hand. 'You must be Nicola Malloy?'

'Yes, that's right.'

'Jane let us know you were coming.' The girl had a freckled face and an engaging smile. 'I'm Sally Granger. I'm the tour nurse. We'll be sharing quarters.'

'That's great,' said Nicola, taking an instant liking to her prospective tent-mate.

'Come and meet the rest of the gang,' Sally invited.

If she had been at all nervous that she would be the outsider in a group of people who all knew each other well, Nicola realised quickly that she'd been wrong, for they were all friendly. There were the men in charge of the horses, Sam and Andy; Craig, whose job it was to manage the supplies; Hank, the guide, and the leaders of two of the smaller groups, Charlie and Edward.

Nicola took the cup Sally handed her and poured herself coffee from the urn. She had just finished telling the group that she'd taken on the job of cook so that she could join the tour, when another man walked into the room. A tall man with dark red hair and an aloof expression.

'Lance!' Sally called to him. 'I'd like you to meet Nicola Malloy. Nicola is our new cook.'

Nicola looked at Lance with interest as they shook hands. His was a name she knew from Todd, for Lance had been a member of the ill-fated little group her brother had led.

His handshake was brief though not unfriendly. Then he asked everyone to sit down so that he could lead the meeting. Nicola listened quietly as he briefed different people on their duties. Mostly, she gathered, what he said was routine, for, apart from herself, they had all been on other tours and knew what was expected of them.

'We fly to the foothills on Saturday,' said Lance. 'The bus that will take us to the base camp will be waiting for us. We'll also meet the tourists and the tour leader there.'

'I wonder who's leading us this time,' Sally said. 'Do you think it will be Gary Simpson?'

'As far as I know,' said Lance. 'Now then, any further discussion?'

There were some questions, a few details to sort out. Lance dealt with everything quickly and competently, but always there was that aloofness in his manner, as if his mind was on other things.

'That seems to be everything,' he said at length. 'See you all on Saturday. And would everyone kindly make : ire that they get to the airport on time?'

Nicola was waiting at the bus stop just a block away from Adventure Tours when a sleek silver Porsche stopped beside the kerb.

'Going home?' someone called.

Her senses leaped to life as she recognised first the voice, then the face leaning sideways towards the open passenger window.

'Why, Jason!' she exclaimed.

'Want a lift?' he asked.

'I might be taking you out of your way.'

A car had stopped behind his, and was beginning to hoot impatiently. 'Hop in, Nicola,' ordered Jason, and she got quickly into the Porsche.

'This is a coincidence,' she remarked, as the car moved into the traffic.

'I was just leaving the office. Were you at the staff meeting?'

'I've just come from there. But I didn't see you, Jason.'

'It's been one of those hectic days. I've been behind closed doors all afternoon. Meeting go all right?'

'Just fine. Everyone is so friendly.' With the exception of Lance, she thought, but he had been aloof rather than unfriendly.

'They'd soon be out of a job if they weren't friendly,' said Jason. 'But you haven't told me, Nicola, are you on your way home?'

'I'm going back to Sea Point, yes. And you haven't told me whether you're going my way.'

He looked at her, and she saw a gleam in the dark grey eyes. 'How could I not be?' he asked drily.

Nicola found she had to look away from him as they turned into Adderley Street. It was only when they turned left towards Sea Point that she felt some measure of calm. Just a few minutes more, and she would be able to say thank you and goodbye to this man who was like nobody she had ever met.

Outside her apartment, Jason stopped the car and turned to her. 'You have five minutes to change into something casual. I'll wait for you here.'

'Don't tell me you're abducting me?'

'The idea is exceedingly tempting.' His gaze lingered sensuously on her lips.

'I'm only teasing.' Her mouth was suddenly dry.

'But I'm not.'

'Jason. . .'

'Actually, I like to go for a run on the beach after work. Will you come with me?'

The sensible thing would be to tell him that she had things to do. But there were times when it was very hard to be sensible.

'I'd like that,' she said, wondering if he caught the

pleasure in her voice. 'But do you usually go to the beach in your business suit?'

'I keep a change of clothes in the car,' Jason told her.

The tide was going out when they reached Clifton, a community a little way beyond the bustling suburb of Sea Point. It was a time of day when there were few people around, so Nicola and Jason had the beach to themselves.

They were both wearing jeans now, and they pulled off their shoes before walking towards the water. Here and there in the soft sand, where children had played during the day, there were sand-castles and an abandoned spade or two. But the damp sand by the shoreline, where the tide had just been, was hard and smooth and unmarked by human footprints. Perfect for running.

'Race you to the rocks!' Nicola said.

'I'm game. How much of a start do you want?'

'You're giving me a head start?' Nicola's laughter was clear and lovely above the sound of the waves. 'I don't need that, Jason. I've never met the man who could run faster than I can.'

'Maybe so. Winner gets a prize, Nicola?'

She stared up at him, and saw the gleam in his eyes. 'Does there have to be a prize?'

'Definitely. It makes the race worth running.'

'What were you thinking of?'

'A kiss,' he said lazily.

Her cheeks were warm. 'A prize without much sense. If you think of it, it would be a kiss either way, whoever wins.'

'Ah, but the winner gets to do the kissing.' His eyes were warm with devilment. 'Therein lies the incentive.'

'I don't know about that. . .'

'I think you're a little scared, Nicola,' he teased.

'Scared?'

'Maybe you've changed your mind about that head start?'

'No way,' she said briskly. 'See, Jason, I'll draw the starter's line right here—for us both.'

They stood at the ready, right feet at the line, right knees bent, left legs stretched back. Then Nicola gave the signal and they were off.

She had run all her life. She'd raced with Todd and his friends, and she'd sprinted at school. Prize after prize had collected on the display shelf in her bedroom. There had never been anybody who could beat her. Yet now, for the first time, on the hard tide-rippled sand of Clifton beach, she wondered if she might have met her match.

At first they ran together, feet hitting the sand at the same level, almost at the same moment. Nicola was running fast, putting everything she had into an effort which had become oddly important. Now and then she allowed herself a glance at Jason, and she saw how relaxed he was. His stride was so easy, as if he was letting her set a pace that he was content to follow.

Twenty feet from the rocks he suddenly sprinted ahead. Nicola was running as fast as she could, but she knew she would not catch up with him. But still she tried, infusing her bare feet with a speed she had not known she possessed.

He reached the rocks just a few seconds before she did. And then he turned and held out his arms out to her.

'You're a great runner,' she said breathlessly. 'You could have won by ten seconds more if you'd really tried.'

'I did try, Nicola.' His hands reached out to cup her face. 'I tried, because I wanted to win.'

The last words were spoken with his head bent and

his mouth so close to hers that she could feel his breath
on her lips. And then he was kissing her. It started as a
gentle kiss, feather-light, just a playful brushing of his
lips around the corners of her mouth.

But then the kiss deepened, and suddenly all playfulness was gone, and there was just a drugging seductive-
ness that made Nicola sag against him as her body turned
to fire. Without thinking, her arms went up to circle his
neck, and her fingers buried themselves in his hair. At
the same time his hands left her face and his arms went
around her back, drawing her body closely against his.

His head lifted at length, and he looked down at her
and said softly, 'Nicola. . .'

She looked up at this most attractive of men. Her
body felt warm and aroused in a way she had never
known.

'You're so beautiful,' he said raggedly.

'Jason. . .'

'Let's go back to my apartment.'

She shook his head. 'I can't.'

'I'll make you dinner this time.'

'No.'

'I promise I won't try to seduce you into my bed,
although lord knows I want to. We'll listen to some
music, and maybe we'll dance.'

The pictures his words evoked were tempting. Much
too tempting.

'I have to go home,' she insisted.

'Please come with me, Nicola.'

Somehow she managed to push herself out of his arms.
'I've a million things to do before Saturday. I'm sorry,
Jason. . .'

He looked down at her, his eyes so thoughtful that she
wondered what was in his mind.

Then they began to walk back across the deserted

beach to the car, and now they were both silent. It was as if suddenly they had nothing to say to each other. More than anything, Nicola wanted to tell Jason that she'd changed her mind, that she would spend the evening with him. But she remained silent.

She knew that she had to part from him now, while she still had a heart left to lose.

It was midday when they got off the plane. A little way beyond the small airport a bus was waiting. The driver was a huge tanned man called Jerry, and, after an introduction to Nicola and warm greetings from everyone else, he stowed their belongings in the hold.

It was not long before the tourists began to arrive. There were thirty of them, men and women of all ages. They came with back-packs and sleeping-bags. All were dressed casually in jeans and T-shirts, and most had cameras slung round their necks. They looked a casual, pleasant lot, Nicola thought.

The new arrivals were welcomed with a friendliness that put them immediately at their ease. Their luggage was also put in the hold of the bus, and then Larry passed around folders containing information about the tour. Name-tags, worn by staff and tourists alike, did away with the need for formal introductions, so that almost immediately people started to get to know one another.

'Except for our tour leader everyone is accounted for,' Lance said eventually, with a glance at his list. 'As soon as Gary Simpson arrives we'll be ready to leave.'

'He's late,' Sally remarked.

'Yes, he is late. It's not like him. I wonder if anything's happened. . .' Lance's words died away, then he exclaimed, 'Good heavens, I don't believe it!'

Nicola's eyes moved in the direction Lance was looking. A tall man, broad-shouldered and with a long, easy stride, was coming towards them, and suddenly her heart thudded violently in her chest.

'*Jason!*' she whispered.

They were all looking at him now, and Sally said, 'Jason! What happened? We were expecting Gary.'

'I know you were.' He was talking to them all, but his eyes were on Nicola. 'Things changed. I'm going to be leading the tour.'

CHAPTER THREE

NICOLA made sure that the big picnic hampers filled with food for the first meal were at the front of the hold, where she could get to them easily. By the time she boarded the bus, tourists and staff had already settled themselves. On every seat except one—which was at the front of the bus and empty—there were two people.

Jason stood talking to the driver. He paused when he saw Nicola, gestured towards the empty seat and said with a smile, 'Will you sit with me there?'

As soon as she'd sat down, Jason picked up a microphone and everyone stopped talking to listen to him.

'Good morning and welcome to Adventure Tours. My name is Jason Langley, and I'm your tour leader.' He glanced around the bus at the faces all turned his way. 'The staff have worked hard to plan a great tour, and we hope you'll all enjoy yourselves.'

A small burst of applause greeted the words, then he said, 'I think what we all want right now is to be on our way. Jerry is our driver. He'll have us at our base camp in about an hour from now.'

'You have such an easy way of talking in public,' Nicola remarked, as Jason sat down beside her.

'I've been doing this for years, remember?'

'I remember that you were going to be leading a tour along the Garden Route.'

'Gary Simpson will be leading it instead,' he told her.

'Why did you swop places, Jason?' she asked him.

'As I said to Sally, things changed.'

'Changed?'

39

'Things happen, Nicola.' There was an enigmatic expression in the grey eyes resting on her face.

A quiver started deep inside her. 'I suppose they do. . .'

'Sometimes we don't know they're going to happen. Could you have known, a few days ago, that you were going to run a race along a lonely beach, and that the prize would be a kiss?'

'How could I have known?' she said through the heartbeats thudding in her throat.

Once more his eyes were on her face. 'That's my point, Nicola.'

She was unable to look at him. Dropping her eyes, she found her gaze riveted to his thighs. It was the first time she had seen Jason in shorts. His legs were strong and muscular, and as deeply tanned as his face and arms and throat. He was so close beside her on the seat made for two that his arm and his thigh rested against hers. Nicola was wearing trousers and a long-sleeved shirt, yet even through her clothes she fancied she could feel the warmth of his skin and the hardness of his limbs.

She managed to tear her gaze away from the disturbing male body and drag it to the window. Had she been able to relax, she would have enjoyed the scenery—the rolling farmlands of the Drakensberg foothills, the cattle and the sheep grazing in the fields, the wild flowers that grew in profusion by the side of the road. As it was, she felt as tense and as tightly wound as a mechanical doll.

Jason's surprise appearance on the tour had made her own situation infinitely more dangerous.

True to Jason's word, about an hour after they'd started they arrived at the base camp. In minutes the tourists had spilled out of the bus and were looking around them with excitement. The staff followed more slowly, their thoughts on their immediate duties. All except Nicola, and she, more tourist than staff, was as excited as anyone.

They were spending the first few nights in this spot. As a Capetonian, Nicola was used to mountains, but the Drakensberg were different from the mountains she knew. Enchanted, she gazed along the line of the escarpment which stretched to the horizon and far beyond on two sides, mountain after mountain folding one behind the next. The lower slopes were like rich green velvet in the sunlight; the upper reaches looked rugged.

A movement caught her attention—a bird, big and black, wheeling and soaring above a high cliff. She narrowed her eyes, shielding them from the glare with one hand, and watched the bird. Was the bridge up there somewhere, with the aloe, and the proof of Todd's innocence?

'An eagle,' said Jason. She had not noticed him come up beside her.

'Will we climb that far?' she asked.

'Eventually.'

'It looks so barren from here, but I expect there's lots to see.'

'You'll enjoy it,' he promised her. 'Look, Nicola, wild flowers everywhere.'

'They're beautiful, and I can't wait to get a proper look at them. But not right now—I'd better think of my job and find the picnic hampers before I do anything else.'

'Another test passed,' he said.

'Oh, what's that?'

'You've just proved you're conscientious apart from anything else.'

He looked anything but an employer as he stood there, smiling down at her. His eyes were warm and amused;

his lips, lifted at the corners, were disturbingly sensuous. It was inevitable that Nicola should remember the kiss he'd alluded to earlier. She just wished that her heart didn't quicken at the memory.

'I'd better get going,' she said reluctantly.

'I've things to do as well,' he said.

He walked away, tall and strong, as superbly built as an athlete, moving over the uneven ground with the easy grace of a man who spent most of his waking hours out of doors. Nicola watched him a few seconds, then she went in search of the picnic hampers.

By the time the lunch—coffee and fruit and sandwiches—was set out, the tourists were starting to get to know one another. The staff helped, making introductions, and inviting those who were a little more reticent than the rest to join the groups that were already beginning to form.

Nicola spent the afternoon getting to know the people with whom she would be working. The more she saw of them, the more she liked them. With one exception, they were a friendly, casual bunch.

Lance was sipping coffee and looking up into the mountains when she saw him.

'Hello,' she said.

His glance was impersonal. 'Hello.'

'We met at the staff meeting a few days ago. I'm Nicola Malloy, the new cook.'

'I remember.'

Feeling awkward now, she said, 'Yes, well. . . This should be a great tour.'

'It should indeed,' he agreed, as his glance moved away from her and back to the mountains again.

Nicola had no time to feel insulted or rejected. The afternoon was passing, and now there were things to do. It was easy enough for Jason to tease her about the tests she had passed. Providing meals for so many people was a big responsibility. It was important that tonight's meal, her first one, should be a success.

And a success it was. Nicola's salads were praised by everyone, and Jason told her the barbecued chicken breasts were delicious.

'I knew you'd cope, Nicola,' he said.

'As long as you don't regret taking me on.'

'Taking you on? Are you asking me or telling me something?' he said, in the lazily seductive tone he sometimes used. 'And is the answer one you don't already know?'

She looked up at him. A gas lamp threw flickering shadows across the rugged planes of a face which, even after such a short time, she seemed to know almost as well as her own. More than anything she wanted to go into his arms.

But when he asked her to go for a walk with him, she told him she was tired. She knew what was happening to her—and she did not want to fall in love with him. If only it did not matter that she was Todd's sister. But she knew it would matter to Jason.

It was quite late by the time Nicola and Sally began to get ready for bed. They were in their sleeping-bags when Sally said, 'Hey, Nicola, did you know you're quite a hit with the men? They all think you're awfully sexy.'

Nicola couldn't help laughing. She had known from the start that she would get on well with Sally. 'Thanks for the compliment!'

'All except Craig. He thinks you're sexy too, of course, but he isn't allowed to say so.'

'I had the feeling you two had something going,' said Nicola.

'Yes, we do,' Sally said softly. 'We met on a tour a

while back and we clicked right away. We've been together ever since.'

'Are you engaged?'

'Yes, we are. We hope to get married next year.'

'That's wonderful! I can understand why you'd fall for Craig. He seems so nice.'

'He is. They all are really.'

'Except for Lance,' Nicola said thoughtfully.

Sally looked at her. 'Why do you say that?'

'He seems so aloof.'

'He tends to be silent,' Sally agreed.

'I tried talking to him, but without any success.'

'Lance is a bit of a loner, Nicola. That shouldn't matter to you. The rest of the men will be fighting for your favours.' Slyly Sally added, 'If Jason lets them.'

'*Sally!*'

'Come on, Nicola, don't sound so astonished. You must have noticed that Jason likes you. He made quite certain you'd be sitting next to him on the bus.'

'There was only one empty seat,' Nicola pointed out. 'And we were the only two not yet sitting.'

'Lance was going to sit there, until Jason asked him to sit with Hank.'

'Really?' said Nicola, over a feeling of quite intense happiness. 'I didn't know that.'

Nicola was up long before her alarm went off the next morning. Slipping on a warm angora sweater and a pair of jeans, she crept quietly out of the tent where Sally was still sleeping.

Nobody was in sight as she went to the kitchen tent. Short of making the coffee and putting the pancakes on the griddle—which she would do when the camp came to life—she did all she could to prepare for breakfast. She also made the picnic lunches. Then she went outside.

The cold mountain air hit her and she shivered, but she did not crawl back into her tent. Instead, she drew the collar of her sweater up high around her chin, and walked a little distance beyond the tents. Beneath her feet the wild grass was wet with dew, and here and there shimmering webs of moisture clung to leaves and twigs.

The escarpment looked quite different in the half-light of early dawn. Thick grey swirls of mist clung to the high peaks, so that a stranger, coming on the view for the first time, would not have known there were mountains.

A little way up the slope she saw a clump of aloes, and she stopped to look at them. Did Todd have pictures of them? It was hard to tell, for in the dawn light they looked grey. Everything in sight looked damp and shrouded and grey.

'You'd never know these were red, would you?'

'*Jason*!' She jerked around. 'I didn't hear you.'

He grinned at her. 'Sorry about that, I didn't mean to creep up on you from behind. What are you doing up so early anyway?'

'I was awake, and I thought I'd get things ready for breakfast.'

'Talk about being industrious! It'll be ages before our lot are all ready to eat. You don't have to get up so early next time.'

'I love it!' Her eyes sparkled. 'There's a holiday feeling out here in the open.'

'Then I won't ask if you're sorry you took on so much responsibility.'

'I wouldn't have missed it! I think I'm going to like being the camp cook.'

'You're quite a girl,' he said softly.

'Wait till you've tasted more of my cooking before you say that,' she teased. 'You might change your mind.'

'Unlikely.'

Once more she had the sensation of things moving too fast. It was time to change the subject. Dancing him a smile, she said, 'Will I have to take your word for it that these aloes really are red?'

Jason laughed. 'Check on them when the sun comes up and see if I was right.'

'I will. It's a good thing I brought along my guide-book. I've a feeling I'm going to be needing it.'

'Actually,' said Jason, 'if you'd been on one of our previous tours you wouldn't have needed it at all.' She saw him frown. 'One of our gudes was a real expert.'

Carefully, Nicola asked, 'Is there no expert on this tour?'

'Oh, sure. Lance is the one who'll take the botany hikes.'

'He's an expert, then?'

'Yes, he is. Many of our guides are students, often graduate students working in a field that's in some way related to the things our tourists are interested in.'

'That's what I thought.'

'But there's nobody quite like Todd. There wasn't a thing he didn't know about the flowers and trees and grasses that grow in these mountains. And he had a gift for putting across what he knew in such a way that even the most ignorant layman couldn't help being fascinated. Which is why it's such a shame. . .' He stopped.

'A shame?' prompted Nicola, hoping the deliberate lightness of her tone hid her tension.

'Todd did something highly unprofessional,' Jason said grimly. 'The consequences could have been very serious. We had to get out a rescue party and there were people who had to spend an uncomfortable night out in the open. Fortunately there were no injuries.'

She had to give herself time to think. 'He isn't on this tour. . .'

'There's no way I'd have allowed him to come again. No other tour company will take him on either. Nor will the university where he was hoping to get a lectureship.'

'Jason——' she began.

'I'm sorry I mentioned his name. Todd Armstrong ruined the last tour. I don't need the memory of what he did to ruin this one as well.'

'But you did say. . .whatever happened. . .there were no injuries.'

'That isn't the point. I trusted Todd. I thought of him as a friend. And all the while he was just thinking of his ambitions. When someone abuses your trust, Nicola, it hurts.'

'I suppose it does,' she admitted.

'I don't want to talk about him any more,' he said. 'Besides, I want to show you something.'

Tension had created an uncomfortable knot of pain in Nicola's stomach. All she wanted was to get away from Jason, to go back to her tent where she could regain some measure of control before she had to go and make breakfast and greet tourists and staff with a smile.

But Jason was holding his hand out to her, it was evident he wanted her to take it. To refuse would be suspicious.

'Yes, all right.' Reluctantly, she put a stiff hand in his.

'Your hand is icy,' he said. 'Put the left one in your pocket. I'll warm it when I've finished warming the right one.'

She had made a fist, and he covered it with his palm. Then he coaxed her hand open, and his fingers laced through hers. His thumb began a slow stroking movement along the top of her hand. Tense and unwilling though she was, Nicola felt something deep and physical come to life within her at the contact.

They had walked about ten minutes when they came to an outcropping of rock. Still holding her hand, the left one now, Jason led her to the front of it.

'There,' he said.

For the first time Nicola realised that they were on the edge of quite a steep slope. Above them was the mist, but below them it had cleared, so that they could look all the way down into a valley. Not fifty yards away a stream fed into a waterfall.

'What a sight!' she exclaimed.

She stepped beyond him, so that she could see further down the slope.

'Careful!' In an instant he was beside her, his arm around her waist, steadying her. 'Don't fall.'

'If you lose the cook, there'll be no more meals for the duration,' she teased.

'And naturally all that interests me about you is your cooking.' He was teasing too, but his voice had the sound of a caress.

'I'm all right,' she said unsteadily. 'You don't have to hold me. I'm good with heights.'

'I want to hold you. You must know that by now, Nicola.'

So saying, Jason turned her in the circle of his arm. He was standing with his thighs against a rock now, and on the steep slope, with the ground falling away just inches from them, Nicola had no option but to lean her body in against his.

The feel of his hard thighs pressing against hers was so incredibly erotic that she forgot the fact that things were moving much too fast with the man who had become her brother's enemy.

As he drew her towards him, excitement was a wild

thing inside her, so that she was ready for him when he began to kiss her. This time there was none of the playfulness there had been on the beach. His kisses were searing, searching, demanding a response that she yearned to give. Driven by the need to be close to him, she gripped his shoulders and her fingers moved in the hair that curled above his neck.

As one drugging kiss merged into another, she lost all ability to think rationally. There was only the mutual exploration of lips and tongues, the ecstasy of his hands moving over her body. She jerked in shock when he slid a hand beneath her sweater and moved up towards her breasts, but she did not pull away from him. They were kissing all the time that he caressed her, one breast, then the other, his fingers spreading fire wherever they touched.

Nicola had long since stopped thinking of Todd and the consequences of what she was doing with Jason. There was just the awareness of the steep slope at her feet, and the heat of her body and that of the man with whom she was rapidly falling in love. All she wanted was Jason.

It was the sound of distant voices that eventually pulled them both back to sanity. They drew apart, looking at each other in a kind of shock. For a while they had forgotten that a world existed outside of themselves.

'You're so lovely,' Jason said raggedly.

'Jason. . .'

'I'd like to take you to a secret place, where we could be alone and nobody would ever find us.'

But for Nicola sanity had returned, and she knew that that place could never exist for them. Not for her and Jason, who would always be on different sides where Todd was concerned.

'We have to go back,' she said unsteadily. 'People will be wanting their breakfast.'

'We'll find that secret place, Nicola.'

'We really do have to go back.' By the second she felt more appalled at what she had allowed to happen.

'It's true—we have to go back. But I don't mind, as long as we find a way of being together.'

He did not seem to notice that she did not answer him. Fifteen minutes later they were back at the camp.

Nicola's first breakfast went off as well as her supper the night before. Her pancakes received rave compliments. One man came back for three helpings, because they were so delicious, he said.

'Better than any previous cook's,' Craig agreed, and Sally gave him a playful shove in the ribs and warned him not to get too used to Nicola's *haute cuisine*, because he would not be getting pancakes in bed after they were married. 'Perhaps I should marry Nicola instead,' he said, and received another shove for the comment.

With two minor exceptions, they were going to be an easy, pleasant bunch to cater for, Nicola decided. The exceptions were Martha and Henry Baynes. A little older than the others on the tour, they had already given her a run-down on the foods they did not care for. Pancakes were greasy and fattening, Martha said. Nicola heard her out, then made them each a lightly boiled egg instead.

'You handled that well,' said Jason, who had over-heard the Bayneses' complaint.

'Isn't there a policy about keeping customers happy?'

Jason laughed, and touched her cheek in a quick caress. 'Within reason. Just see that Martha and Henry don't boss you about too often.'

The interests of the people on the tour ranged from bird-watching to geology to an enthusiasm for bushman art. There were some, like Nicola, who were eager to learn more about the profession of mountain flowers and shrubs. And then there were the others, with no special interests at all, who just came along for the fun of the tour, and who joined whichever group happened to take their fancy on any particular day.

Nicola finished her kitchen duties in time to go hiking. Lance was the leader of the botany group, and as they were about to leave the camp Jason said he'd decided to join them as well.

They first stop was at the aloes which Nicola had seen earlier. 'They really are red!' she exclaimed, pretending astonishment.

Jason laughed. 'I had a feeling you didn't believe me.'

'Some things a girl has to see for herself.'

'Why wouldn't they be red?' Lance asked.

'Just a joke,' Jason said.

There was something rather lovely about sharing a private joke with Jason. Nicola was smiling as she focused her camera and took her first photo.

It was the first of many photos taken that day, for there were flowers everywhere: tiny ones massed on the ground, bigger ones lifting their heads above the dry grass. Now and then they came upon an aloe or a protea, huge flowers with waxy-looking leaves and stems. Nicola's camera clicked constantly.

At times they stopped and Lance would say a few words about a particular plant. His manner was a little dry, even a bit pedantic, but Nicola had to admit that his knowledge was extensive.

The sun was high in the sky when they stopped in a small meadow and ate the picnic lunch Nicola had prepared for all the groups. Shortly after that it was time to turn back. It was mid-afternoon when they reached the camp, and Nicola hurried to the kitchen tent.

★ ★ ★

That evening they had a *braaivleis*. One of the men lit the fires, and by the time Nicola brought out huge platters of steak, *boerewors* and *mielies*, the first high flames had died down and the grids were ready.

It was dark long before they were finished eating. Craig put some new logs on the dying embers, then settled back with his arm around Sally. The companionship of the day had loosened the tongues of people who had thus far exchanged only pleasantries. In no time at all there was a party atmosphere around the fire.

Jason went to his tent and came back with his guitar. He sat down beside Nicola and for a while he strummed quietly, creating a background of harmony to the conversation all around him.

After a while Sally said, 'Let's have a sing-song,' and Jason played the chords to a traditional camp-fire song which everyone knew and loved. There was another song, and then another: camp-fire songs, folk-songs, and rounds which had people laughing when the harmonies went wrong.

Nicola, a little light-headed and more than a little tired after the long day out of doors, had to fight the urge to lean her head against Jason's shoulder as she joined in the singing.

And then they started something different. Going around the circle, each person had to make up the words to a solo nonsense verse. After each verse, the whole group clapped and sang a simple chorus together:

> 'Tra-la-la-la-la-la-la-laaa,
> Tra-la-la-la-la-laaa,
> Tra-la-la-la-la-la-la-laaa,
> Tra-la-la-la-la-laaa!'

The camp staff, who were all old hands at the game, had their own special verses. But the tourists rose to the occasion and joined in too. Even Martha Baynes, who insisted she couldn't manage a single line, came up with a verse that was very funny. And after every verse came the chorus.

'Tra-la-la-la-la-la-la-laaa. . . .'

And then it was Nicola's turn. She was more tired than she had realised. It was just as well that a verse, ready-made, popped into her mind.

> 'I have a little shaker,
> It makes me wheeze and wheeze,
> 'Cause it is filled with pepper
> And always makes me sneeze.
> There is this tight-rope dancer
> Who loves to dance and tease.
> She took it to the circus
> And sneezed from the trapeze.'

At the end of the verse she waited for the chorus. There was silence. No one sang. The strumming of the guitar ceased abruptly. The staff all stared at her. The tourists looked around the circle, confused and uneasy, understanding that something had happened, not knowing what it could be.

Beside Nicola, so close to her that she had been aware of his whipcord hardness against her body all evening, Jason had gone rigid.

'I don't understand. . .' faltered Nicola.

It was Lance who broke the terrible silence. 'That was Todd's verse. Nobody else ever sang it.'

CHAPTER FOUR

NICOLA heard an exclamation and the hiss of Jason's indrawn breath. Stiff with shock, she glanced around her. The firelight showed her the dazed looks of the tour staff.

'You didn't tell us you knew Todd,' said Lance.

'I suppose it never came up.' It was an effort to speak.

'But it did,' said Jason, so quietly that nobody except Nicola could have heard him. 'Several times, in fact.'

She had no idea what to say. Her head throbbed with the combined effect of fatigue and distress. The cursed fatigue that had loosened her tongue and blown her cover.

'I have a headache,' she said, as she got unsteadily to her feet. 'I. . . Excuse me.'

She was almost at her tent when Jason caught up with her. At the sound of his footsteps she jerked around.

'So, Nicola. Running away, are you?'

'*No*!'

'What made you leave the fire?'

'I told you. . .I have a headache.'

'You seemed perfectly all right until a few minutes ago. It must have come on very quickly,' said the Jason who, in the space of a few minutes, had turned into a cold, angry stranger.

'It did. Look, Jason. . .I'll see you in the morning.'

'We'll have a talk first. In my tent.'

Alarmed, she said, 'I'm off to bed.'

She tried to move past him into the tent, but he blocked her way.

'I really do want to go to bed, Jason.'

His hand seized her wrist. 'When we've had our talk.'

She was silent a moment, feeling the steel in the hand that gripped hers.

'We can talk here,' she said then.

'In my tent, Nicola. Where we won't be interrupted by Sally or anyone else walking this way.'

'Jason. . .'

'Come along, Nicola.' The steel was in his voice too, and the words were an unmistakable order.

'All right, then,' she said, injecting into her tone a calmness that she was far from feeling. 'But let go of my wrist. You're hurting me.'

His tent was the furthest one from the fire. At the entrance he parted the flap and waited for her to walk in first. He came in after her and motioned to her sit down on a camp stool.

She watched him turn up the light of his gas-lamp, and waited for him to sit down beside her. But he remained standing. The effect was intimidating.

'Start talking, Nicola,' he ordered.

It was time to be assertive. 'You brought me here, so why don't you start? And while we're about it, would you please sit down.'

'I prefer to stand.'

'It would be a lot friendlier if we were on the same level. I find it disconcerting to have someone glaring down at me.'

'I think you know that I don't feel in the least friendly towards you at this moment, Nicola. Stop playing me for a fool, and tell me about Todd.'

'Jason——' she began.

'And don't try telling me his name never came up. You and I talked about him this morning.'

'That's true,' she admitted.

'What are you to Todd, Nicola?'

'His sister.'

Jason looked down at her sombrely. 'I should have known! The first day I saw you, there was something about your eyes. They struck a chord, and I couldn't think why.' His lips tightened. 'I brought it up then. I asked if we'd met.'

'I remember,' she said faintly.

'You could have told me the truth, but you deliberately chose not to. Instead, you gave me a silly story and an invented name. Nicola Malloy. Why didn't you tell me your real name was Nicola Armstrong?'

'Because my name really is Nicola Malloy. I'm only Todd's half-sister. We had different fathers.'

'Supposing I accept that part,' he said after a moment, 'what about the rest of it?'

'What do you want to know, Jason?'

'You were so darned eager to come on the trip. So eager that you were even prepared to sign on as cook when you found out the tour was booked up. A photographic model who wasn't in the least concerned if her hands became rough from all the kitchen work. All that nonsense about having a bit of leave and being mad about flowers! I should have taken you for a phoney from the start. Why didn't you tell me the truth?'

'Would you have taken me on if you'd known who I was?'

'Of course not.'

'There's your answer, Jason. I detest lying—I never do it as a rule—but I knew you wouldn't consider me the moment I mentioned Todd's name.'

'In other words, you lie whenever you're unable to get your own way,' he said contemptuously.

'I don't lie!' she said angrily. 'I've just told you that. In this instance what I did *was for Todd*, and it was a very special situation. Besides, I didn't actually tell any lies.'

'I've no patience with hair-splitting,' he said contemptuously. 'You didn't tell the truth. That's all that matters.'

Nicola fought back the tears that welled in her eyes. 'I can understand that you're angry.'

'You have no idea quite how angry I am. How could Todd put you up to a stunt like this?'

'It wasn't Todd——'

But Jason went on blindly, ignoring her words. 'Is your brother so ambitious that he'll let nothing stand in his way? First he concealed the warning sign—now this. He knew I would never allow him to come on another tour, so he pushed his sister into conning me instead. All of it so that Todd Armstrong can have what he wants!'

'I don't think you heard me, Jason—this was *my* idea.'

'*Yours?*'

'Todd was reluctant to let me go,' she explained.

'Then why did you?'

'You must know how hard my brother has worked on his book. How badly he needs photos to illustrate it. He dropped his camera bag with all his spools when he fell off that bridge.'

'And you thought it would be a sisterly good deed to take new ones.'

Nicola lifted her chin at him. 'That's right.'

'One photo in particular.'

This time she remained silent.

'The purple aloe,' Jason said harshly. 'The wretched purple aloe that could have ruined the reputation of my company. Does Todd never give up?'

'Don't you understand? It was *my* idea to come on this trip.'

'Your brother risked the safety of his group to find that flower.'

'*He did not*! And that's the other reason I came. To see if I can find out the truth about what happened at the bridge.'

'Todd moved the sign.'

'No, Jason, he didn't!'

'Face it, Nicola—it was there. We found it the next morning, lying in the bushes. Todd moved it because he was so dead set on finding the aloe that he wasn't going to let anything get in his way. Not even a sign warning people that the bride wasn't safe to walk on.'

'That's not what happened!' she cried. 'Why won't you believe him?'

'Because the evidence was there. I'm sorry—Todd was my friend—but I have to say that he was prepared to endanger the group for what he wanted.'

'That's not true, Jason! It isn't!'

He looked down at her a long moment. His eyes were narrowed, thoughtful. His lips were a hard, firm line. 'I'm afraid there's no other explanation.'

Nicola had known there would be grief if she were to let herself fall in love with Jason. This was the hard and angry man Todd had known when things had gone wrong. Her brother had tried to warn her.

'Are you going to stand in my way?' she asked.

'I won't allow another disaster,' Jason said crisply.

'Nothing will happen,' she promised.

'Nothing will happen because I won't permit it. I'll be watching you, Nicola, every moment. If you step out of line I'll know how to deal with you.'

She was shaken by the bitterness in his voice. 'You're so angry,' she whispered.

'Angry! I told you, you don't seem to understand quite how angry I really am.'

'All because you don't believe Todd.'

'Actually, that's the least part of it.' His voice grew harsher still. 'I'd have thought you'd know that, Nicola.'

Her throat was tight. 'I know you're upset because I lied to you.'

'Of course I am. But what I really don't understand is why you kept up this whole stupid charade later.'

Suddenly she was trembling. 'Later?' she echoed.

'You knew I was attracted to you.'

'Jason, don't——'

'You said our evening together felt more like a date than a test. It *was* a date. Why in heck do you think I took you out dancing? Because I wanted to hold you in my arms, that's why. And the kiss on the beach. . . You must have realised that I planned to pick you up at that bus-stop so that we could spend some time together. Did none of it mean anything to you?'

'Jason, please——'

'Nicola, please,' he mocked. 'You must have known. Of course you did. And you were amused. The guy you were conning was actually falling for you. What a joke! How you and your precious brother must have laughed when you told him about it later!'

'It's never been like that,' she whispered.

'And to top it all, I got Gary Simpson to switch places with me.'

'You did that because of me?' She was trying to hard not to cry. 'I didn't know.'

Jason bent towards her suddenly and gripped her shoulders in his hands. The movement brought her up from her sitting position. 'I wanted to get to know you better. Stupid, wasn't it?'

She shook her head, acutely aware of his closeness, of her breasts and hips against his body. 'No. . .'

'Yes, my dear, it *was* stupid. I was married once—did your brother tell you that?'

'He said your wife couldn't accept the life you lived.'

Roughly Jason let her go, so that she fell backwards on to the chair. 'It was more than that. She betrayed my trust. I won't go into the details, they don't concern you. Sufficient to say that I was shattered. Afterwards. . .when I'd got over Serena, I resolved never to be hurt again.'

'I would never hurt you, Jason,' Nicola told him in a low voice.

'You won't have an opportunity to. I thought we might have something going for us, Nicola. No chance of that after tonight.'

'You really hate me,' she said painfully.

'I have nothing but contempt left for you.' His voice was as hard as she had heard it.

She felt ill. 'If I hadn't sung that silly verse you'd never have known,' she muttered.

'The verse wasn't important. The truth would have come out sooner or later anyway, if only when Todd's book was published and I saw the photos and his acknowledgements. He did mean to acknowledge you, didn't he?'

'I never thought about it. Jason, you never answered my question—are you going to try and stop me taking photos? Your can't! I won't let you.'

'Todd doesn't deserve a sister like you.' He had not softened exactly, but there was something, the slightest hint of admiration, in his tone.

'Then you will let me do what I came here for?' She allowed herself a slight bit of hope.

'I meant what I said about watching you. Step out of line even once, and you'll have me to deal with. And don't expect any mercy from me, Nicola.'

★　★　★

Nicola did not look at Jason when she left him. From the camp-fire came the sound of singing, but she walked towards her tent. Drifting cloud covered the moon, making the night so dark that she was glad she'd remembered to bring a torch to light up the uneven terrain.

It was some time later that she heard Sally and Craig whispering their goodnights. She opened her eyes when Sally came into the tent.

'Did I wake you?' her friend asked apologetically.

'I wasn't asleep.'

'The sing-song went on longer than usual. We've a keen bunch on the tour with us this time, they couldn't seem to get enough. I think they'd have been happy to sing all night.'

'I'm relieved that verse of mine wasn't a complete dampener,' said Nicola drily.

'It was a bit of a surprise,' Sally admitted.

'*A bit*? You all looked so shocked.'

'I suppose we were. At that moment, anyway. It was a little unexpected, Nicola.'

'Am I going to be ostracised by you all from now on, Sally?'

'Heavens, no! Why would you think that?'

'Jason is furious,' Nicola told her.

'Well, yes, I suppose he would be.'

'He can't get over the fact that I didn't tell him the truth.'

'You have to remember that the accident darkened the last tour,' Sally reminded her.

'I'm totally condemned in his eyes, Sally.'

'Give him time, Nicola. He'll get over it.'

'I doubt it.' Nicola was quiet a moment. Then she asked, 'Do *you* think what happened was Todd's fault?'

'I've never known what to think,' Sally said honestly.

'The evidence was rather damning. But I want you to know, I liked Todd.'

They were talking about him as if he'd been written off, as if he were dead. And in a sense he was, for with the accident all his hopes and dreams of a career had been shattered.

'Do you think I did something dreadful?' Nicola asked. 'Coming on the tour under false pretences, so to speak?'

'On the contrary, I admire you for what you did. I know Craig does too. I'd like to think I'd have the courage to do the same for someone I loved.'

Warmed by the words, Nicola said, 'I'm beginning to wonder if I did the right thing.'

'You can't doubt yourself at this stage, Nicola.'

'There's still time to go back.'

'*Nicola*!' Sally stared at her.

'Jason and I talked. I told him I was going to take all the pictures I wanted. That I was going to find out what really happened at the bridge that day.'

'Well, then——'

'Now I'm suddenly beginning to have second thoughts. We haven't gone all that far. I could find transport. Jason could find another cook.'

'Is that really what you want?' Sally asked.

'No, of course not! But I'm not sure I can remain here with Jason hating me.'

'You haven't made up your mind, have you, Nicola?'

'Just about. I know Todd wouldn't hold it against me if I went back. He'd be far more upset if I remained here under pressure.'

'I'm not going to try and influence you one way or the other,' Sally said. 'But why don't you think about it a little longer before you make a decision?'

* * *

Long after the sound of Sally's slow breathing filled the tent, Nicola was still awake. Too restless to go on lying in her sleeping-bag, she got up after a while, pulled on jeans and a warm sweater over her pyjamas, and walked quietly out of the tent.

It had grown colder in the last hour or so, but the temperature did not bother her as she walked a little way up the path she and Jason had taken early that morning. All around her the mountains were great black humps against the cloudy sky. The shrilling of the crickets was a harsh, unceasing sound, and the air was pungent with the scent of the mountain shrubs.

There was a huge rock by the path. Nicola stopped and leaned against it, staring into the blackness of the escarpment. Below her, she knew, was the lovely scene Jason had shown her that morning. Above her was the unknown, all the places the tour would explore. On these mountains were the plants Todd loved, the wax-leafed aloes and the proteas, the dainty wild flowers, the cacti and the shrubs.

This was Jason's world. It was Todd's world. It could be Nicola's world too. And suddenly she knew the answer to her problem.

Going back home would be a cop-out, the easy solution to her problem. What she had said to Sally was true: Todd would understand. There would be not a single word of reproach from him. He had not wanted her to come in the first place, he would not hold it against her if she returned. The fact was she had come on this trip for a double purpose.

Whether Jason liked it or not, she meant to accomplish it.

Despite her sleepless night, Nicola was up early again the next morning. Jason's sarcastic comment about the model ruining her perfect hands had rankled. Determined to prove to him that she took her duties seriously, she had the picnic lunches ready and packed before anyone stirred in the camp. By the time tourists and staff arrived for breakfast, the trestle-tables were laid, and pancakes, sausages and coffee were ready. She had even remembered Martha and Henry Baynes' soft-boiled eggs.

Jason took his place in the queue with everyone else. Like the others, he held out his plate to Nicola for pancakes and sausages.

'Morning,' he said. And then, 'Thank you!' His only words, spoken so curtly that he might as well not have said anything at all.

When everyone was eating, Nicola poured herself coffee—she could not bear the thought of food today—and joined Sally and Craig at the table furthest from where Jason was sitting.

'I'm glad you've decided to stay,' said Craig.

Nicola flashed a quick look at Sally, who said comfortably, 'Don't worry, I've talked to nobody except this man of mine.'

'I liked Todd,' Craig told her. 'I'd like to think that what happened wasn't his fault.'

Nicola felt tears spring to her eyes. 'Just knowing I have friends means a lot to me,' she said gratefully.

After breakfast Jason addressed her again. This time he wanted to know what arrangements she had made for the picnic lunches. Again there was the correctness of the boss talking to the employee. Not a personal word of any kind, not even a mention of their argument. Nicola felt cold inside, but she hid her feelings with a manner as impersonal as his.

During the next hour she had some contact with most of the staff. All were friendly, though in a cautious kind of way.

The only one who really surprised her was Lance.

She was cleaning up in the kitchen tent when he approached her and said, 'I've been looking for you, Nicola.'

She looked at him warily. 'Did you want me to prepare something special for the hike?'

To her amazement, he was smiling. 'You've done that already. Actually, I was wondering if you'd like to join my group again today.'

'I might. . .'

'We're almost ready to go, but we can wait till you're done here.'

Still surprised, she looked at him. 'That's very nice of you.'

'In case you're wondering,' he said, 'I have an idea Jason may be going with one of the other groups today.'

'Oh. . .really?'

'I hope you don't take my mentioning that as presumptuous.' He looked a bit troubled. 'It's just that after what happened last night. . . We all saw Jason follow you when you left the fire. I can guess that whatever was said was not pleasant.'

Nicola shifted her feet on the sandy floor of the tent. She was in no mood to discuss Jason with Lance, of all people.

And so she was even more surprised when he said, 'Todd was my friend. I liked him. I also admired him enormously. It's such a shame that he lost his pictures.'

'It *was* a shame,' she agreed.

'I suppose you'll be taking new ones for him?'

'That's the idea.'

'He'll still manage to turn out a fine book, I'm sure of it.'

'It's more than the book, Lance,' she said, beginning to warm to him, 'it's his whole career. Before all this happened, he was almost sure he'd get a position at the university.'

'I know. . .' Lance paused, then said, 'It's none of my business, of course, but are you going to try and find the purple aloe?'

'If I can.' He was turning out to be so unexpectedly sympathetic that she decided to confide in him. 'At the same time, I mean to find out what really happened at the bridge that day.'

'You don't believe Todd hid the sign?'

'I *know* he didn't,' said Nicola earnestly.

'He wanted very badly to get across the bridge, Nicola. It would have been the high point of the tour for him.'

'I know that. I also know that he would never have dreamed of endangering the group.'

'You could be right. . .' he agreed slowly.

'Can you think of anything?' she asked.

He stared at her. 'What do you mean?'

'Something you might have seen or heard. . . Something that could lead me to find out the truth about what happened?'

Lance shook his head. 'There's nothing I can think of.'

'The smallest clue would be valuable.'

'I realise that. But there's nothing—I mean, nothing apart from the way we all know it happened.'

'The official version,' she said.

'It's the only version I know. I'm sorry.' He stood looking at her a moment. Then he said, 'But look, if there's anything I can do to help—anything at all— please tell me.'

'You're very kind.' She was touched.

'I told you Todd was my friend,' he said. 'I want to help him every bit as much as you do.'

* * *

Lance was wrong about one thing. Jason *was* in the group that day. Nicola came close to backing out of the hike when she saw him, hard-faced and steely-eyed, waiting with the others.

And then Lance flashed her a reassuring smile and said, 'Camera all loaded and ready?'

Ignoring Jason, she said, 'I've just put in a new spool.' She looked around, still without meeting Jason's eyes. 'I hope I didn't delay anyone. I was busy in the kitchen tent until a few minutes ago.'

Lance made it mercifully easy for Nicola to keep away from Jason. He was always pointing out things the group might miss: a tiny cactus here, thrusting its way out of the ground between a cluster of rocks; an innocuous-looking shrub with a lovely aroma there; an exotic flower concealed behind a mass of long underbrush somewhere else. Yet through it all, he seemed always to remember Nicola's presence, and the photos she was after.

Once he said softly, almost as if he did not want Jason to hear him. 'See the proteas up there? Aren't they beautiful? If you want take a few pictures, I'll slow down the rest of the group till you catch up with us.'

He did indeed keep the others distracted, so that they had only walked a little way by the time she reached them. Again in an undertone, Lance told her the name of the plant she had photographed, and advised her to write it down against the number of the photo in her camera spool. This would be a great help for Todd later, when it came to developing film and sorting the pictures, he said.

All day it was the same. Not a shrub or a flower which Lance did not point out, not a name he did not seem to know. Not an opportunity for a photograph which he let slip Nicola by. He was the total opposite of Jason, who ignored her completely.

They were almost back at camp when Jason spoke to her for the first time. 'You must have shot a whole spool today.'

'More than one spool,' she told him.

'And you think your brother will be glad?' His eyes glinted in a way she did not understand.

'I know he will be.'

'Don't forget your real role on this tour, Nicola.'

She lifted her chin at him. 'Do you have any complaints?'

'Not yet.'

'You say that as if you expect that you will have.'

'If I do, you'll hear from me,' he said flatly. 'Don't ever forget it, Nicola.'

They had a *braaivleis* again that night, and a camp-fire. No sing-song this time, though. Instead, a circle game was begun, with each person telling his or her funniest experience.

Jason was nowhere near Nicola tonight. He sat between two female tourists, who seemed to be enjoying his company immensely, she noticed grimly.

But Nicola was not alone, for Lance was at her side all evening. He stood beside her while they were barbecuing their meat, he helped her pass around plates and serviettes and cutlery, and he insisted on helping her with the cleaning up. Afterwards, he sat beside her at the camp-fire.

By ten o'clock people had begun to drift towards their tents. Jason was among them. Nicola, tired after the long day, started to say goodnight too, but Lance reached for her hand when she tried to get up.

'Don't go yet,' he said.

'It's getting late, Lance.'

'This is the best part of the day.'

'It's lovely, but if I'm not up early I'll hear about it from Jason.'

'Just a little longer.' He reached for some wine and poured her a glass. 'Come on, Nicola. It's such a beautiful evening.'

He was making it difficult for her to say no. 'Well, all right, just a bit longer,' she agreed.

The wine was delicious. It was a semi-sweet Riesling made from grapes that grew far south in the Cape, and in the cool night air it had the taste of champagne. When Lance pressed another glass on Nicola she could not refuse. She tried to resist when he put his arm around her and drew her head against his shoulder—something inside her cried out for Jason—but Lance was persistent, and the wine seemed to have made her a bit light-headed.

The small group at the camp-fire broke up eventually. It was just as well that Lance walked Nicola to her tent, for her legs were suddenly so weak that she might not have managed without his arm around her waist, and her head felt very heavy.

Somehow she made it into the tent where Sally was already asleep. In the morning she could not remember taking off her clothes and getting into her sleeping-bag.

'Wake up, Nicola!'

'Ugh. . .' The word was an indistinct groan.

'*Come on, Nicola!*'

There was a bad taste in her mouth and her head was like lead. Her eyelids were as heavy as if someone had placed weights on them to keep them closed.

'Who. . .? Why. . .?' she muttered.

'Don't tell me you're drunk!' The words were said with such disgust that they got through to her.

'Not drunk,' she protested.

'Sure looks like it. It's late, Nicola. You have to get up.'

'Want to sleep, Sally.' Why couldn't her tent-mate leave her in peace?'

'You can't sleep now, and I'm not Sally.'

Not Sally. . . Who, then? Nicola's eyelids lifted a fraction in sudden alarm.

'Jason!' It was a groggy exclamation.

'Are you going to get up?'

'What. . . what are you doing here?'

'I came to get you up. Breakfast should have been started ages ago.'

'I'm so tired.' Her eyes closed again.

'That's too bad, isn't it? You've nobody to blame but yourself if you choose to spend the night carousing.'

The evening by the camp-fire was beginning to come back to her.

'Three glasses of wine,' she said shakily. 'That's all I had.'

'For a person who can't take wine even three glasses is too much. Surely you must know your own limits?'

'But Lance. . .' She stopped. 'Where's Sally? Why didn't she wake me?'

'Because she was called out some time ago to see Henry. He wasn't feeling well during the night.'

'I'm not feeling well either.'

'Well or not, Nicola, it's time you got up.'

'I can't. . .'

'Then you can consider yourself fired.'

'*Fired*?' Her eyes opened wider this time.

'You heard me.'

'Jason, no!' she protested.

'As of now.' It was too dark in the tent to see his eyes, but the expression on his face was hard and unsympathetic. 'Pack your case, and I'll drive you to the nearest town.'

'No!'

'You can make your way back home from there.'

'You don't mean it!' gasped Nicola.

'Absolutely. Your brother ended his employ with me because he endangered the lives of his group. You're going the same way because you've proved yourself to be irresponsible.'

She could not lose the job. Not with Todd depending on her.

'What's the time, Jason?' she asked.

'Almost seven.'

'I'll make breakfast,' she said grimly.

'Are you up to it?'

'Yes.'

'You don't have much time.'

'I'll do it. You can leave me now.'

'I want to see you get up,' he said grimly.

'No. . .'

'Get moving, Nicola!'

She tried to sit up. She really tried. For some reason she could not make it. She was falling back on her pillow when Jason caught her.

'Steady now.' The tent spun before her eyes, and she was too dizzy to hear the slightly softer note in his tone.

'I can manage on my own,' she said.

'Can you really?'

'Yes,' she said, and he left the tent.

At least Jason was gone. She would have to manage now, even if at this moment she was uncertain how she was going to do it. By sheer force of will Nicola levered herself up. The tent spun once more, and she put a hand to her aching head.

She was sitting on her sleeping-bag, hands supporting her head, when Jason returned.

'Don't you ever knock?' she asked weakly.

He laughed softly. 'I doubt you'd be in a position to answer if I did. And how do you knock on a tent, anyway?'

It was the first time she'd heard him laugh since her fiasco at the sing-song.

'Here,' he said, 'I think you can do with some help.'

'Don't need help,' she muttered.

'You're in no state to refuse it, Nicola. So you may as well give in with good grace.'

She flinched when the wet wash-cloth touched her face. 'My God, Jason,' she cried, 'it's freezing!'

'It'll wake you up,' he said, as he proceeded to wipe her forehead and her cheeks.

'You really are a cruel man!' she gasped as the wet cloth touched her throat.

'All I ask is that it wakes you up.'

'I'm awake. Get out of here, Jason. I'll be dressed in no time.'

'And here,' he said, ignoring her protests, 'is something to clear your head.'

She saw the cup in his hand at the same moment as she smelled the pungent aroma.

'I don't think I could swallow a drop,' she said weakly.

'It's good coffee. And you can drink it if you try.' He put the cup to her lips. 'There now, Nicola, just a sip.'

She made herself swallow a few drops. It wasn't as bad as she'd expected.

She tried to reach for it. 'I can hold it.'

But the cup eluded her as Jason moved it away from her hand. 'I prefer to hold it,' he said.

'Why?'

'Seems safer that way.'

Sip by sip, Nicola drank the coffee until the cup was empty. Her head really did seem a little clearer after that. She looked up at Jason.

'Better?' he asked.

'Much. I'm OK now.'

'I think you are. What made you do it, Nicola? Why did you drink all that wine?'

'Lance and I were at the fire. There were a few of us. We were talking, and I suppose we were just being companionable.'

'Lance gave you the wine?'

'He didn't know I couldn't take it. I didn't know myself.'

'He'll know better than to give you so much after this—I'll make sure of that.'

'It wasn't his fault,' she said quickly.

'I'm aware of that. Now then, let's see if you can stand.'

'You will not watch me get dressed,' she said firmly.

'Don't taunt me,' he said, and, taking her hands, he pulled her to her feet.

She was standing, and he was still holding her hands. They stood just inches apart, and she looked up at him, about to tell him to go. In the same moment her grip tightened and his head bent towards her.

His kiss was hard, a bit possessive. Yet a moment after she began to kiss him back he pulled away from her.

'What was that all about?' she whispered.

'It happened. It wasn't meant to.'

'Jason. . .' She ached to go back into his arms.

'Nothing has changed. So just forget it, Nicola.'

'How can I?'

'You have to,' he said harshly. 'Because it didn't mean a thing. Not a damn thing.'

'Jason, please. . .' She took a step towards him.

But he had turned away from her, and was walking quickly out of the tent.

CHAPTER FIVE

'NICOLA'S no good with wine,' said Jason a little while later.

'I don't understand,' Lance said.

'She had too much of it last night.'

'I don't think she could have had more than a few glasses.'

'Evidently a few more than she seems able to handle.'

Lance stared after Jason as he strode away. Then he turned to Nicola. There had been no time for pancakes today, and she was scrambling a great batch of eggs instead. On the surface her hands looked steady enough, so that nobody—save for Jason, and now perhaps Lance—would have guessed that each movement was planned and deliberate.

'You don't have a hangover?' Lance looked shocked.

'In a way.'

'Not after that tiny bit of wine. You couldn't have, Nicola!'

'I'm afraid so,' she admitted.

'Good lord! I don't believe it! Are you all right?'

'I am now.'

'I don't know what to say. . . A few glasses of wine. . . I never dreamed this would happen.'

'Don't think about it,' Nicola told him. 'I should know my own limitations, and I'm certainly old enough to say no.'

'It won't happen again,' Lance said firmly. He looked enormously troubled. 'There's something else I don't understand—how did Jason know?'

74

'When he missed me in the kitchen tent, he came looking for me. Unfortunately, he had a bit of trouble getting me to wake up.'

'Was he angry?'

'Furious. So much so that he tried to fire me.'

Lance seemed to jerk. Then he said, 'That's terrible!'

'Fortunately he changed his mind,' she told him.

'Just the thought. . .'

'The point is, it won't happen again, because if it does, Jason really will fire me. I have no illusions about that,' Nicola said grimly. 'I had a purpose in coming on this tour, and nothing is going to keep me from accomplishing it.'

'I should hope not!'

'Look,' she said gently, 'you really shouldn't be so upset. Please don't be. Not on my account.'

'How can I not be upset? I would never have forgiven myself if you'd been sent away just because I persuaded you to join me in a bit of wine.'

He was so nice, so concerned about her. So different in every way from Jason.

'You'd have had nothing to forgive yourself for,' she said, in the same gentle voice. 'I really wish you'd forget it. Especially as I'm going to make quite sure that it doesn't happen again.'

'All right.' But the concern was still in his eyes. 'Hey, Nicola, I have an interesting hike planned for today.'

'I think I'll give it a miss,' she said.

'But there'll be such wonderful plants for you to photograph. I know Todd would love them.'

'I'll have to try and get them some other day.'

'But, Nicola. . .'

'I'm not up to it, Lance. To tell you the truth, I still feel a bit groggy. I don't think I could walk very much further than my tent.'

'I'll make an excuse,' he said. 'The others can go on their own and I'll stay here with you.'

'No, don't do that.'

'You shouldn't be left alone.'

'You're so nice,' she said, putting her hand briefly on his arm. 'You're such a kind man, and I appreciate it. But believe me, I'll be fine alone. All I need is a few hours of sleep.'

'If you're sure. . .' Lance did not look convinced.

'Quite sure,' she assured him.

Washing the dishes and cleaning the kitchen tent seemed like a marathon chore that morning. Nicola's head still felt thick, it was an effort to move her limbs. It was only by sheer force of will that she managed to do what she had to.

Once she looked up, and saw Jason watching her from the entrance.

'Are you all right?' he asked.

Nicola heard his impersonal tone. Unlike Lance, he was not concerned about her welfare. Not any more. Jason only wanted to be certain that the efficient organisation of the tour would not be disrupted.

She nodded. 'I'm fine.'

'You'll have dinner ready on time?'

'Naturally. Why do you ask?'

'In the circumstances, I'd think you could hardly blame me for wanting to know.'

She flashed him an angry look. 'I may be a bit woozy this morning, but that doesn't make me an all-out drunk! Of course dinner will be ready on time. Tonight and every other night.'

'Just checking,' he drawled.

'I won't give you a chance to get rid of me, Jason.'

He looked at her, his eyes hooded, but he did not

come back with a quick answer. In a way his silence and that strange unreadable look were more unnerving than any sarcastic words might have been. The one thing that was clear was that Jason had not given another thought to the kiss an hour or so earlier. He had spoken no more than the truth when he'd said that the kiss had meant nothing to him.

Without another word he left the tent, and Nicola went back to her chores. Groggy though she was, she tried to infuse her movements with a measure of energy. While there was any chance that Jason might check on her again, she was determined to give him no cause for criticism. It was only when she heard the different groups leave the camp that she let herself relax.

She was surprised when someone else entered the kitchen tent. This time it was Sally.

'I've been busy till now,' her friend said briskly. 'Tell me what I can do to help you.'

'You don't need to do anything at all,' Nicola protested.

'I want to. Don't you think I feel bad enough letting you oversleep the way you did? Here, give me a towel, and let me start drying. And after that I think you should get into your sleeping-bag.'

'Thanks,' Nicola said gratefully, as Sally took the dishtowel. 'I feel such an idiot, Sal.'

'Don't be silly. You're not the first person to wake up with a thick head.'

'The strange thing is, I didn't have more than a couple of glasses. How can anyone be hung over after that?'

'Some people have a lower tolerance level than others.'

'But I'm not a child, Sally. And it's not the first time I've had wine.'

'Maybe the wine combined with all the sparkling

mountain air was too much for you,' Sally teased cheerfully. 'Stop thinking about it, and let's get done here.'

Twenty minutes later Nicola was back in her sleeping-bag. No pillow had ever felt so good beneath her head. When she emerged from her tent a few hours later, she felt ready to face the day.

Sally was sitting in a camp-chair in the shade, knitting a sweater for Craig. She smiled when she looked up and saw Nicola.

'Feeling better?' she asked.

'I feel wonderful!'

'Good. Do you know, I've been thinking, Jason probably misjudged you. It could be that what you had was a touch of a twelve-hour bug of some kind. These things often go as quickly and mysteriously as they come.'

'I'd certainly feel less of a ninny if I thought that was the cause all along,' Nicola admitted.

'You could tell Jason that was what it was.'

'I have a feeling he wouldn't care either way. Not at this stage, anyway. All he wants is a reason to get rid of me.'

'You don't really believe that.'

'I've never been more serious. The thing is, I won't give him that reason. Say, Sal, I'm starving!'

Sally laughed. 'You really are yourself again!'

They made themselves coffee and a few cheese and tomato sandwiches, then they walked down to the stream that ran along the slope a little way from the camp. It was lovely there, with the sun warming their bare arms and legs, and the water rippling clear and clean over shining stones.

A flat rock made a good place for a picnic. After they had eaten, Sally picked up a couple of pebbles and sent them skimming neatly over the surface of the water.

'You're quite an expert,' Nicola said admiringly. 'Any time I try skimming pebbles they sink to the bottom the moment they touch the water.'

Sally grinned. 'Craig taught me. And long enough it took me too to get the knack of it! You could say our courtship was measured by my progress in skimming pebbles—one ripple, then two and three. Craig wasn't satisfied until I could manage a whole long row of them. Seems he sees it as a necessary skill in the future mother of his children.'

She sent another pebble dancing across the water, then she turned and looked at Nicola. 'Talking of court-ships—you seem to have made quite a conquest of your own.'

'Jason doesn't care about me any longer,' Nicola said painfully. 'I though you knew that.'

A look came and went in Sally's eyes, as if she'd caught a glimpse all at once of something she had not expected.

Then she said, quite gently, 'Actually, I was thinking of Lance.'

'Lance?' echoed Nicola.

'His attentions couldn't have escaped you.'

'It's true, he is very attractive,' Nicola said slowly. 'He's always by my side, and he puts himself out to help me get good photos. And you should have seen how upset he was over what happened this morning.'

'Well then!'

'I don't think you could call it a conquest. I mean, for the first little while he didn't even seem to know I existed. I'd try talking to him, and he'd look right through me with that aloof expression he has so often.'

'We talked about that, remember? But he certainly knows you exist now.'

'Yes. . . And yet it's strange, Sal. He seemed to notice

me only after I sang Todd's verse. His attitude changed when he knew I was Todd's sister. Just as Jason——' Nicola stopped.

A moment passed. Then Sally said, 'Whatever the reason, I think Lance could be getting serious about you.'

'I'm quite sure you're wrong,' Nicola said firmly. It was enough that she should spend every waking moment yearning after Jason. She needed no additional complications in her life. 'Lance told me he was Todd's friend. Apparently he was very upset by what happened at the bridge. I'm convinced he's being nice to me *because* I'm Todd's sister.'

'You could be right.' But Sally did not sound entirely convinced. 'I've known him a long time, and I've never seen him so attached to anyone.'

'And now you know why,' said Nicola.

It was so pleasant by the stream that they could have sat there for hours, but by mid-afternoon Nicola decided it was time to go back to the campsite.

In the kitchen tent she cut pieces of lamb, green peppers and onions into cubes. Then she speared the cubes on to skewers, alternating the meat with the peppers and onions. When the voices of returning tourists sounded outside, she made a huge mound of fried rice into which she threw herbs and spices and tiny pieces of canned pineapple.

Compliments on the meal were profuse. Martha Baynes even put in a request for a repeat *sosaties* meal, and Lance told Nicola she had excelled herself.

The only person who said nothing was Jason. At this point Nicola expected no compliments from him, so she was suprised when he spoke to her later.

'Nice meal, Nicola.'

The simple words meant more to her than all the other

more extravagant compliments she'd received. Her cheeks were warm as she looked up at him. 'Thank you,' she said.

'Seems you do know how to cook after all.'

She threw him a provocative look. 'You sound surprised.'

'I am a bit.'

'Even though I passed a test?'

'In the light of all that's happened since then, you can't blame me if I was beginning to wonder,' he told her.

'Jason. . .' she had to ask the question, 'does this mean I'm forgiven?'

'Let's just say that tonight's meal made up for what happened this morning.'

There was a lightness in his tone—a touch of amusement—which gave her hope.

'I meant more than this morning,' Nicola said quietly.

'Oh?'

A little hesitantly, she asked, 'Are you still angry with me?'

Even in the dark, she could feel his gaze on her. After a moment he said, 'I think you're asking if I've accepted the fact that you conned your way on to the tour?'

'Yes. . .'

'I can't accept that. I never will.' The amusement had left his voice.

'Jason——' she began.

'I hate lies and deception. I loathe not being able to trust someone I like. I especially loathe it when that person is a woman I could have——' He stopped. When he went on his voice was harsh. 'I'm saying too much. The fact is, as far as my feelings about your deception are concerned, nothing has changed.'

* * *

It was time to move on. After breakfast the next morning—a very early breakfast in the damp grey light of
dawn—they left the base camp for a new camp higher
and deeper in the escarpment.

There was no bus this time. Where they were going
there was a trail but no tarred road. Sam and Andy had
risen a few hours before the others, and the horses were
saddled and ready. There was a horse for every member
of the tour, and there were pack-horses which would
carry personal belongings and provisions.

It was a lively group which left the base camp. So far
the tour had been a great success. People generally were
happy with all the things they had seen thus far. In
Nicola's tote-bag were two rolls of finished spool and a
long list of names and notes. She could not wait to see
Todd's face when he saw what she had brought him.

'Aren't the horses unusually frisky this morning?' a
nervous voice asked.

Nicola looked at the woman riding beside her. Anthro-
pology was Linda Shelton's hobby, but until this tour it
seemed she had learned most of what she knew from
books and pictures. Her expression was so habitually
anxious that Nicola wondered sometimes whether Linda
ever regretted having seen the Adventure Tour's bro-
chure and her decision to join the trip.

She smiled at Linda. 'They do seem a bit frisky, don't
they? Must be the cool morning air.'

'You look so comfortable on a horse,' said Linda.
'Have you done a lot of riding?'

'A fair amount. My brother taught me years ago. We
used to ride through the forests and along the beaches.
How about you?'

'I'm really a novice. In fact. . .' Linda bit her lip
'. . .I hate to admit it, but I took my first lessons only
after I decided to come on the tour.'

'You seem to be managing really well,' Nicola remarked.

'I'm not sure. . . I keep wondering if it will get a lot more difficult.'

'Shouldn't think so,' Nicola said cheerfully. 'The horses won't want to gallop up these steep slopes. Our only problem may be a little saddle-soreness when we reach the next camp, and Sally will have a remedy for that.'

'I suppose so. . .' Linda looked only slightly reassured.

Nicola was about to distract her with more conversation, when Jason rode up alongside her, wanting to know what arrangements she had made for lunch and supper. His horse was moving more quickly than hers, so she coaxed her own horse to keep pace. Yet even as she talked to Jason, she made a mental note to keep a check on Linda's progress.

'You seem to have everything under control,' Jason said.

Nicola threw him a look. 'I keep telling you I won't give you a chance to fire me.'

'So that's the reason for your diligence. Planning meals when you'd far rather be busy with your camera!'

But his tone told her he was teasing, and inside her was a warm feeling she could not prevent, for she had given up trying not to love Jason.

Now and then Nicola looked behind her. Linda was a little behind the rest of the group. Her body was stiff and her brow was furrowed in intense concentration. Once she saw Nicola looking back at her, and her lips moved in the merest hint of a smile.

The trail became stonier, narrower. The horses' hoofs made clicking sounds against the stones beneath the underbrush. Nicola leaned forwards to help her horse when the slope was steep. She was glad that the pack she carried on her back was light; she had brought only a blouse and shorts to change into later, when the sun grew hot. The rest of her belongings would reach camp with the pack-horses.

Again she looked back. Linda had fallen even further behind the others, but she was still in sight. Her body was more rigid than ever now, and she no longer responded to Nicola's smile. She would tell Linda how well she had done when they stopped for lunch, Nicola decided.

Further they went, and higher. They came to a stream, and the horses crossed it. And on they went.

There was a sound. A cry. An exclamation of some sort. Nicola could not have said exactly what it was or who uttered it. She looked around her, then behind her down the slope.

Linda was on the ground by the stream, a hundred yards back. It looked as if she was getting out of the water. Her riderless horse was moving away from her to join the rest of the group.

In a moment, and without a word to anyone, Nicola had turned her own horse and was guiding it back down the slope.

Linda was crying when she reached her. Nicola reined in her horse, jumped quickly to the ground, and put her arm around the weeping woman.

'Linda! Are you all right? Are you hurt?'

'My hand. . .' sobbed Linda.

Nicola looked at the graze where Linda's hand must have scraped a rock. It was dirty, but she did not think it was serious. Other things concerned her more.

'Did you hit your head?' she asked urgently.

'No.'

'How about your back?'

Linda had stopped crying. 'I'm all right. It's just my hand. God, I feel such a fool!'

'Anyone can fall,' Nicola said in relief. 'What happened?'

'We were crossing the stream, and the horse stumbled.'

'It fell?' Nicola asked, concealing her surprise, for the mountain horses appeared to know their territory so well.

'No, it didn't fall. But crossing on those rocks there— the slippery ones—it seemed unsteady.' Linda looked at Nicola. 'Does that sound silly?'

'No, because I know just what you mean. The stones *are* slippery, and the horses do skid about a bit sometimes.'

'I guess that's what happened. I wasn't able to stay in the saddle. I don't know why. . . I just rolled right off into the water. At least it's shallow up here, so I didn't have too much trouble getting out of the stream.'

Nicola could picture exactly what had happened. 'You're shivering,' she said.

'The water's icy.'

'It would be! Here, take my jacket.'

'I can't do that!'

But Nicola was already peeling it off. She was putting it around Linda's shoulders when Jason came riding down the slope. In one hand he held the reins of Linda's horse.

'What happened?' he asked, as he jumped to the ground.

'I fell.' Linda put her hands in front of her eyes. 'I feel so *stupid*!'

Nicola looked up at Jason. 'I've told Linda it could have happened to anyone. Her horse stumbled as it was crossing the stream.'

Linda dropped her hands. 'You're very kind. But I shouldn't have fallen. It's not as if the horse fell. If I were a better rider I'd have stayed in the saddle.'

'Nicola's right,' said Jason. 'You mustn't think like that. I want to know if you're hurt.'

'My hand. . .' Linda faltered.

'I'll go and get Sally. She'll see to it.'

But Sally was already far ahead with the rest of the group. And for Linda's sake, the less fuss, the fewer people who knew about the mishap, the better.

Nicola stopped Jason as he was about to ride back. 'I can do it,' she said.

'Sally has the emergency kit.'

Nicola let her eyes slide briefly but deliberately in Linda's direction. She did it in such a way that only Jason could see the look. 'We don't need it. This isn't an emergency, it's just a graze. Sally can bandage it properly later—if she thinks it's necessary.'

Jason hesitated. 'Maybe. . .'

'Is the water clean?'

He would know she was asking him about bilharzia, the scourge that lurked in so many African rivers. But bilharzia was most often to be found in stagnant water. This water was cold and fast-flowing and clear.

'We're quite high up here, so yes, it's clean,' he said. 'I had it checked quite recently, and I know it for a fact.'

'Good. Do you have a handkerchief, Jason? No? I don't have one either. How about you, Linda?'

Linda shook her head, and Jason said, 'Perhaps I really should get Sally.'

'No, Jason, don't.'

'But, Nicola——'

He stopped as Nicola stood up, drew her shirt from her waistband, tore a strip from the hem in one swift movement, grinned at him, then went to the water.

Crouching on a rock, she bent and dipped the torn scrap in the icy water. Then she turned back to Linda.

'I'll try not to hurt you,' she said, as she took Linda's hand.

The graze was red and raw-looking, but it was not bleeding. Nicola washed away the tiny bits of sand and grass and grit which were embedded in the skin. Linda flinched once, but after that she was still.

When the hand was clean, Nicola looked up. 'Was that very bad?' she asked.

'Not the way you did it. You're so gentle.'

Beside them, Jason moved his feet. Nicola had been aware of him watching her all the while she was attending to Linda, but she had not allowed herself to look at him.

'Now for a bandage,' she said.

'Sally will give us one,' said Jason.

'We need something makeshift in the meantime. Linda won't be able to hold the reins without something to cover the graze.'

They were both looking at her, Linda with wonder, Jason with speculation in his eyes. Amused suddenly, Nicola grinned at them both, and tore another strip from her blouse.

'Nobody would give me a nurse's certificate on the basis of this bandage,' she teased, when she had tied the torn cloth around Linda's hand.

'I feel better already,' Linda said gratefully.

'You're still shivering. You'll feel even better when you've changed into some dry clothes,' Nicola said. 'Let's get your back-pack.'

'It looks wet to me,' Linda said doubtfully.

They opened it. Inside the pack Linda's clothes were wet through.

'We've a long way to go,' Jason said grimly. 'You can't go on in this wet stuff.'

'She won't have to,' said Nicola. 'We're about the same size. My clothes will fit you, Linda.'

Linda looked shocked. 'I already have your jacket. I couldn't possibly take the rest of your things!'

But Nicola was insistent. 'I have a blouse and shorts and a light sweater. I want you to wear them.'

'You'll be uncomfortable when it gets hot, Nicola.'

'I'll change into something cooler when we get to the next camp. I'll be fine until then.'

'I think you'd better do as Nicola suggests,' Jason put in. 'You'll get sick if you go on in those damp clothes.'

'I don't know what to say.' Linda gave Nicola another grateful look. Then she vanished behind some bushes to change her clothes.

Nicola sat down on a rock, and after a minute or so Jason sat down beside her. He was so close to her that she could feel the warmth of his body, could sense the muscularity of his arms and legs.

'Nicola,' he said softly.

Her pulses began a sudden hard racing inside her. 'Yes?' She kept her eyes turned away from him.

'Look at me,' he said.

Slowly, painfully, she turned her head and looked into his eyes. He was so close to her that she could see the little flecks that warmed them. Jason put an arm around her shoulder. With his other hand he touched her cheek, very lightly. His fingers moved around her mouth, tracing its contours, stopping between her lips in a kind of finger kiss.

'Thank you,' he said.

'For what?'

'For coping.'

'It was nothing,' she shrugged.

'I wouldn't say that.'

The hand moved lower, brushing downwards over her

throat, sending a trembling excitement spreading through her body. The arm around her shoulder tightened. She could feel his breath on her face, and she knew he was going to kiss her. She closed her eyes.

At that moment there was the sound of a horse on the slope. Nicola opened her eyes as Lance rode into view.

'What on earth is going on here?' There was a strange wide-eyed look in Lance's face as his glance went from the three tethered horses to Nicola and Jason, sitting so close together.

'Nothing serious,' Jason said. 'Get back to the group, Lance. We'll be along in no time.'

But Lance was looking at Nicola. 'Suddenly you were gone. Someone said they'd seen you riding back this way. And then you were gone too, Jason.'

'There was a slight mishap,' Jason explained. 'Linda fell off her horse into the stream.'

'Good lord!' exclaimed Lance.

'Nicola heard her cry out. By the time I realised what had happened, she was already helping Linda.'

'I'll stay and help too.'

'I'd prefer it if you went back to the others,' Jason told him.

'You might need me.' There was an odd tension in Lance's voice.

'Please go, Lance. And not a word about what happened. Linda doesn't need any more embarrassment.'

Jason spoke with an air of authority that was unusual for him. Lance looked from one to the other, his expression as tense as his voice had been. Then he wheeled his horse round and rode it very quickly back up the slope.

Nicola sat still as she watched Lance go. Beside her, just barely touching her arms and her legs, was the long, hard length of Jason's body. If she could have one wish granted, it would be that he would kiss her. He had been about to kiss her in the moment before Lance had arrived, she was certain of it.

But the mood had been broken. Jason sat a moment longer, then he stood up abruptly. He was looking at his watch when Linda emerged from the bushes wearing Nicola's clothes.

'You look much better,' he said.

'I feel fine.' For the first time Linda was smiling.

It was a smile that vanished when Jason said, 'Then I think we should move on. I'd like to catch up with the rest of the group.'

'I can't get back on the horse,' Linda said faintly.

Jason looked stunned. 'You can't walk.'

'Please. . . Please don't force me!'

Nicola threw Jason a quick look, before turning to Linda. When she spoke it was gently but firmly. 'You have to ride, Linda.'

'I can't!'

'Yes, you can. You will.'

'Let me walk. I'll catch you up.'

'No.'

'I'll find you, I know I will,' Linda insisted.

'I want you to ride, Linda.'

'I can't! I was frightened before, but now. . .'

The woman had become a child, pleading, scared. Nicola's heart went out to her, but she knew that she had to remain firm.

'For your own sake you have to get on the horse,' she said. 'We understand that you're frightened, but if you get right back on now you'll get over your fear, I promise you.'

'I don't think I can. . .'

At least it was not a flat refusal this time. Nicola darted a look at Jason.

'We'll help you, Linda,' she said.

'How?'

Nicola looked once more at Jason. 'Will you lead my horse a while?'

He nodded.

'Then I'll hold the reins of your horse, Linda, and I'll walk beside you. At least until you feel confident once more.'

Linda looked doubtfully at them both. 'I'm really sorry,' she said. 'I should never have come on the tour. I should have known that a few riding lessons would never be enough.'

Jason smiled at her. 'That's nonsense. You fell— we've all fallen at some time or another. By the time we get to the end of the tour you'll be a seasoned rider. Now come along, let me help you on to the horse.'

It was a slow procession that made its way up the slope. Linda sat on her horse tensely as Nicola walked beside her, one hand on the reins. A little ahead of them, Jason led his horse and Nicola's.

They had gone about a quarter of a mile in this fashion when Linda looked down at Nicola. 'I'll be all right now,' she said.

Jason stopped to listen as Nicola said, 'Are you sure?'

'I think so.'

'I don't mind walking a little further with you, Linda.'

'I'm fine. I didn't think I would be, but I am. You did the right thing, making me get back on the horse.'

Jason looked at Nicola as she reclaimed her horse. Experienced rider that she was, she did not need a hand up, but he gave it to her anyway.

'You did well today.' He spoke so softly that Linda, a few yards back, could not have heard him.

'Thank you.' Her voice was equally soft.

'In some ways you're a most remarkable woman, Nicola Malloy.'

He moved away from her then. But she had seen the warmth in his eyes, and suddenly it did not matter that they had been disturbed when he'd been about to kiss her.

CHAPTER SIX

THE rest of the group was in sight just a little way ahead when Nicola turned to Linda. 'Maybe you'd like to take off the bandage?'

Linda looked at her in surprise. '*Now?*'

'We're going to be stopping for something to eat, and then Sally will be able to disinfect the graze.'

Linda glanced down at the ragged piece of red shirt material covering her hand, then back at Nicola. 'That way nobody would ever know. . .'

'Not that it's important,' Nicola said. 'Anyone can fall off a horse.'

'It may not be important to you and Jason—you're both so understanding. But I'm not so sure about some of the others. I don't know what someone like Graham might say. . . I'd rather no one realised I had the nerve to come on the tour when I barely knew how to ride.'

Graham was a tough, outgoing man who looked more like a cowboy than an anthropologist. Nicola had never realised Linda's interest in him, but, knowing it now, she could understand why Linda would not want to look weak in his eyes.

'Your riding is fine,' Jason assured her. 'I don't know if you know it, but you seem more confident now than when we set out this morning.'

'I *feel* more confident.' For the first time that day Linda actually looked happy. 'And it's all due to the two of you. If you hadn't forced me to get back on the horse I'd have lost my nerve altogether. Now. . .maybe it's silly, but I think I can cope.'

'You can thank Nicola for that,' said Jason, with a smile in Nicola's direction, and for the second time that day she felt absurdly happy.

But she did not let herself dwell on it. 'If you do decide to take off the bandage, it would mean riding the rest of the way using only your right hand. Do you think you can do that, Linda?'

'It's such a short distance. . .' Linda lifted her chin. 'I know I can do it.'

She took off the makeshift bandage and stuffed it into the pocket of the shorts Nicola had lent her. Minutes later they had rejoined the group.

As Nicola had expected, there were only a few curious questions, and Jason fielded them casually, with not a word about Linda's mishap. They'd been delayed, they hadn't realised the time. It was really no big deal, and everyone seemed to accept it as such. Nicola noticed that Lance's face was stiff with disapproval, but it was obvious that he had said nothing to the others about Linda's fall, just as he did not correct Jason's account now.

'This is a good place and time for a break,' Jason said, and the announcement was greeted with enthusiastic approval. After a long morning's ride everyone was ready for a rest and a snack.

Lance was at Nicola's side, his hands around her waist as she dismounted. 'You shouldn't have stood by while Jason ordered me back,' he said.

She looked at him in surprise. 'It was nothing personal. Just that the others would have started to wonder if too many of us were missing.'

'Didn't you realise that I was concerned about you, all alone by the stream?' he asked tensely.

'That's considerate of you, Lance, but I was never alone. Linda was there. And Jason, of course.' She tried to take a step away from him, but his hands were still on her waist, and she didn't want to make too much of a closeness she found she did not like very much.

'You and Jason don't get on together.'

'There are times when we get on very well.' Involuntarily Nicola smiled at the thought of quite how well they had got on that morning.

Lance's hands stiffened and his fingers gripped her fiercely. 'I find that hard to believe.'

Looking up at him, Nicola saw that the strange wild-eyed expression was back in his face. After a moment she said, 'The only reason Jason is angry with me is that I didn't tell him the truth about myself at the outset.'

'Jason is not your friend, Nicola,' he said hardly.

'Lance. . .'

'Don't you know by now that you and he will never be friends?'

'I'm not sure,' she said cautiously.

'It's a fact. Jason isn't the kind of man to be content with one woman. He was married once, did you know that?' And when she nodded, 'Why do you think it didn't last? He's a man who needs the freedom to have many women, that's why.'

She was taken aback by the mutinous expression in his voice and his face. Warm, gentle Lance, so nice always—he was showing her a side of himself she had not suspected existed.

'You do know that I'm your friend, Nicola?' he went on.

'Well, of course I know that. And I'm so grateful to you for all your help. Todd won't know how to thank you enough either.'

It had been the right thing to say. The grip on her waist loosened, and she was able to step away from him.

Briefly she touched his hand and smiled up at him. 'I

have to find Sally. I need to speak to her about Linda before I start with the lunch.'

She left Lance standing there, still with that strange intensity in his face. What had got into him today? she wondered. But she did not have time to wonder for long, because there were things she had to do, and they were important.

Sally was drawing a splinter out of someone's hand when Nicola found her. When Sally had finished, Nicola drew her aside and quietly told her about Linda's grazed hand.

'Of course I'll look at it,' Sally said.

'I tried to clean it as best as I could.'

'I'm sure it's fine. And don't worry, I won't say a word about Linda's fall. Poor thing, I can see why she'd be sensitive about it.'

Nicola's next stop was with Andy. He had organised the pack-horses so often that he knew exactly which one was carrying the day's picnic lunch.

The place where the group had gathered was a small plateau. All about them were the mountains, crowding, closing in on them in a way that was far more dramatic than anything they had yet encountered. Even those who had been here on other occasions were awed all over again by the splendour.

Some of the men began to shout words. 'Hello. . . hello. . .!' And back came the answering echoes—hel-loooo. . . hellooo. . .! They were all calling then—names, greetings, questions. Echoes reverberated all about them, mingling in a kind of indistinguishable thunder.

Nicola would have loved to join in the fun, but now she was conscious of her duties. No matter how warm Jason had been today, she knew there was some truth in Lance's words when he said Jason wasn't her friend.

Every meal had to be good; she could not afford to let down her guard for a moment. She had not forgotten Jason's threat to fire her if things were not done to his satisfaction.

Nicola had risen long before daybreak to prepare the picnic, and judging by the comments her efforts had been worthwhile. The coffee was steaming hot. The sandwiches were cool and fresh, and the biscuits she had wrapped so carefully had lost none of their crispness.

It was a lively crowd that picnicked that day on the plateau. They took photos of the views and of each other, and they laughed and joked right through the meal. Linda looked in as good a mood as the others when she showed Nicola the hand that Sally had disinfected and covered with a plaster.

'Not quite as debonair as the red bandage, of course.' Linda was laughing.

'Not as visible either,' said Nicola.

Lance was the only quiet one in the group. He stayed beside Nicola's side all through the picnic, never moving more than a few inches away from her. He was like a shadow, following her wherever she went. It was as if he was determined that nobody else should seek out her company.

She tried to make conversation with him, but it was hard going. No matter what she said, the strained expression never left his face for long.

'Is something bothering you?' she asked him at length.

'Of course not!'

'But, Lance, you seem upset about something.'

'You're imagining it!' He almost snapped the words.

Wisely, Nicola decided to leave it at that. Something was most decidedly wrong, but if Lance was going to tell her what the matter was, he would have to do so in his own time. Until then she would not press him.

She was glad when Jason said it was time to go on.
When she had mounted her horse she looked around for
Linda, and as they set off she made sure that she
remained close to the other woman. For the most part
the trail was so narrow that the horses had to walk in
single file. But here and there the trail broadened, and
then Nicola was able to edge her horse beside Linda's.

'I wish you could see yourself,' she said. 'You look
great. You're riding so well.'

'I feel great,' Linda said happily.

They were starting to climb once more, and Nicola
said, 'Lean your body forward, not back. Yes, like that.
Easier on the horse, easier on yourself.'

At the top of the slope Linda turned to her. 'I didn't
know. Nobody ever told me. It really is easier this way.
I was so scared of all that steepness, I kept thinking I'd
slide off backwards.'

The path narrowed once more, and Nicola motioned
Linda to ride in front of her. The slope grew steeper,
and Linda leaned in with the horse. She was starting to
ride as well as anyone else.

And then they came to another stream and Nicola saw
Linda stiffen. Once more she made a point of being at
her side. 'You can do it,' she said softly.

'I'm not sure. . .' Linda looked a little scared.

'Yes, you can. It's a tiny stream, there's hardly any
water.'

'The rocks. . . I might fall. . .'

'Relax! Don't try to guide your horse. Let it go. It
knows how to make its way across.'

Nicola crossed the stream first, then reined in her
horse. She did it unostentatiously. Anyone seeing her
would have thought only that she was waiting for her
friend.

At the edge of the stream, Linda stopped her horse.

Nicola saw her eye the rounded rocks beneath the water. Her shoulders were stiff now, the hands on the rein were tight. She looked across at Nicola, who gave her a wink and a thumbs-up sign.

It was enough to give Linda courage. Seconds later her horse began to cross the stream. Barely breathing, Nicola watched. Once, when a hoof slid on a slippery rock, the horse jerked. But Linda remained in the saddle.

Half a minute later she was beside Nicola. 'I did it! Oh, lord, I did it!' Her face was pale and there were tears in her eyes.

'I knew you would.' Nicola reached across and touched her hand.

'It's all due to you. I couldn't have done it without you.'

'Maybe I helped, but you were the one with the courage. You were wonderful. You'll have no problems after this.'

The remainder of the ride was exciting. Through mysterious gorges they went, and along high sunny ridges. Linda was riding with such confidence now that Nicola was able to enjoy every minute. It was mid-afternoon when they reached the alpine meadow where they would sleep for the next few days.

Nicola gazed around her in wonder. The view was majestic. Great peaks rose on all sides, with patches of snow here and there on high shaded slopes. The grandeur of the scene was beyond anything she had expected.

With so much to do before it grew dark she could not linger. Already the pack-horses were being unloaded and people were taking their belongings to their tents.

Nicola rolled out her sleeping-bag and unpacked some of her belongings in the tent she shared with Sally. After that she went directly to the kitchen tent which had already been set up.

Working quickly, she prepared for the *braaivleis*. Though she kept the meals simple, she made sure there was an abundance of food, because people would be hungry after the long ride. Lance hovered around, wanting to know what he could do to help, but Nicola told him that she worked better on her own, and sent him gently on his way.

It was quite dark by the time the flames in the pit had died down, and the coals were grey and ready for the meat. Nicola put steak and *boerewors* and foil-wrapped potatoes on the grids. Then she set out salads and rolls on a big trestle-table lit by the flickering light of two gas-lamps.

Only when everyone had helped themselves to food did she serve herself. She was looking for a spot by the fire when a hand caught hers, and someone said, 'Nicola.'

'Jason. . .?'

'Come and sit with me.'

He reached for her plate and held it while she sat down beside him. For a while they ate in companionable silence. For Nicola their closeness was a vivid reminder of the closeness they had shared earlier in the day.

At length Jason said, 'So, Nicola, what do you think of this place?'

'It's wonderful! Incredible!'

'You didn't know what to expect?' There was a smile in his voice.

'A little. Todd talked about it so often. He loved it so much. . .'

She stopped as it came to her that they had not mentioned Todd's name since the night of their argument.

Beside her she felt Jason stiffen.

Then he said, 'He did love it. He loved it very much. He was never happier than when he was up here in the mountains. And his enthusiasm was infectious. The tourists all took him to their hearts. Everyone wanted to be in Todd's group. Always *Todd's* group. . . That's why what happened is such a darn shame!'

'Doesn't it make you realise that perhaps it didn't happen? At least, not in the way that you think?' she asked urgently.

'But it did. You can't get away from that, Nicola. It happened.'

'I still mean to find out the truth about that day,' she told him.

'You know the truth.'

'I know what Todd told me. What you've told me.'

'It's all there is.'

'I don't believe it! I haven't done anything much yet, because we haven't come to the bridge, and I don't quite know what to do.'

'I do know that you've been talking to the rest of the staff,' Jason told her.

'That's true, I have. There isn't a person I haven't spoken to, but nobody seems to know any more than you do. And wherever I go, I keep looking around, but I never see anything that can help me. Sometimes I feel so frustrated!'

'Maybe it's time for you to stop thinking about it.'

'I can't do that, Jason. I think about it every day. It's one of the reasons I came on this trip.'

'I'm afraid you won't discover anything we don't know already, Nicola. But good luck anyway. I've said it before—Todd is a lucky man to have you for a sister.'

He had turned to her at the last words. She tried to see his face in the firelight. She could not see the expression in his eyes, but there was a softening in the line of his lips, and the stiffness had left his body.

'I didn't ask you to sit by me so that we could talk about Todd,' he said then. The softening was in his voice too.

'Really?'

'I started to tell you earlier—before we were interrupted—how good you were with Linda.'

'I didn't do anything out of the ordinary,' she shrugged.

'In my eyes you did.'

'I cleaned her hand. Anyone else would have done the same.'

'That much, yes. But you didn't have to tear your shirt or give her your clothes. And your patience in getting her back on the horse. . . You showed great kindness and sensitivity.'

'Thank you.' His praise caught her off guard. She was glad it was dark, so that he could not see the sudden tears that filled her eyes.

'I liked the way you suggested she take off the bandage before we reached the others,' Jason added.

'I wasn't sure I did the right thing there.'

'You did—I should have thought of it myself, but I didn't. We've quite a rugged bunch on this tour, Nicola. And while anyone can fall off a horse—is there anybody who's never done that?—Linda was right. Some of them would have looked down on her for coming on the trip when she barely knew how to ride. Graham could be one of them.'

'That's what I thought. . .'

'And you went on helping her afterwards. I noticed that you kept close to her after the picnic. I saw you coaxing her over the stream.'

'That's all she needed—a little bit of coaxing,' Nicola explained.

'Maybe. But I wanted you to know that none of it has gone unnoticed.'

The words gave Nicola the same lovely warm feeling she'd experienced at other times when she and Jason were getting on well together. If only there was a way of making the peace last!

'By the way,' she said mischievously, 'did you notice Linda is sitting with Graham this evening?'

'I did.' Again there was that smile in his voice.

'Until today, I didn't even realise there was anything between them.'

'Do you think,' Jason said very softly, 'that anyone realised there'd been anything between us at the beginning of this tour?'

Her heart thudded hard inside her as she turned to look at him. 'I don't know. . .'

He was silent a few moments. When he spoke again the softness was gone from his voice. 'The pity of it is how quickly relationships change.'

'Did this one have to change?' The question made it with difficulty past her lips.

'You can ask me that?' She could feel him staring at her through the darkness.

'I only thought. . . After all the nice things you said about Todd. . .'

'None of that changes what he did. Or your own deception, Nicola.'

'Jason——' she began.

'Don't you think I wish with all my heart it didn't matter? You're so lovely—the loveliest woman I've ever known. But I was lied to once. Unfortunately I know only too well what it means when you can't trust the person closest to you. I can't—*I will not*—go through anything like that ever again.'

If there was an answer, Nicola did not know what it was. Jason had made up his mind about her, and at this stage it seemed unlikely that he would ever change it.

There were times when conversation flowed so freely between them, almost as if one picked up the other's thoughts even before they had been spoken. But Jason's last words seemed to put an end to casual talk, at least for the moment.

They sat side by side, staring into the flames, neither talking to each other nor taking part in the lively discussions all around them. Overhead the sky was a brilliant mass of stars, and the night air rang with the interminable sound of the crickets.

A little way from the fire, a few of the tourists began the echo game once more.

'Strange how different the echoes sound at night,' Nicola said, because she had to say something or be driven crazy by the strained silence.

'A bit eerie?'

'That's it! You throw out a word, and you never quite know in what form it will return to you.'

'All you know is that it won't sound the same as when you said it.'

'Right,' Nicola agreed.

'In a way it's the same with feelings,' Jason said.

'I don't understand. . .'

'You take a gamble when you feel strongly about someone else. You show your feelings, but you don't know in what form they'll come back to you.'

'That's rather a profound thought,' Nicola said with deliberate lightness.

'Don't you think there's some truth in it? You know your own feelings—or you think you do—and you show them. But what comes back to you can be quite different.'

'It can also be the same.'

'That doesn't happen often,' said Jason.

'Sometimes you have to play the game to know how it will turn out.'

'The problem is,' he said, 'that sometimes it turns out that the game was the wrong one to play in the first place, and then you're sorry you ever started.'

'That can happen too, I suppose.' A dull pain was beginning to form in Nicola's chest.

'And perhaps you never really know what the outcome will be until the game is over,' Jason added.

'Perhaps not.'

The fire was burning low. It was chilly now, chillier than it had been at the lower elevation of the first camp. A few people were beginning to go to their tents. Nicola shivered.

'I think I'll turn in,' she said.

'It's early.'

'It's cold.'

His arm went around her. The contact was so unexpected that her body jerked.

'Does that feel better, Nicola?'

'Yes.' She did not look at him. She could not.

They were silent once more. And yet, despite all that unnerving talk about echoes and feelings, it was a different silence from the last one. The arm around Nicola's body had a lot to do with it. The warmth it imparted, the sense of two bodies sharing the same space. The fact that it was Jason's arm and not someone else's. For there it was—she loved him. And nothing he said or did seemed to change that fact.

Craig started a sing-song. Sally handed out marshmallows and pointed sticks. Jason speared two sticks, held

them over the fire, and gave one to Nicola when the
marshmallow was toasted. It was delicious, charred on
the outside, soft and sticky within.

They had sung a few songs when someone started the
nonsense verse game, and, as on that one fateful night,
everyone had to sing an individual verse.

Nicola's turn came, and for a moment she hesitated.
Then, in a sweet, clear voice, she deliberately sang
Todd's verse. There was a small silence when she
reached the end then someone laughed.

'You're a provocative hussy,' Jason whispered against
her ear.

'You'll have to take me as I am,' she whispered back.

'Do you know,' he said slowly, 'there are times when
I'm sorely tempted to do just that.'

It grew later, colder. The remaining people began to
think of their sleeping-bags. Jason walked with Nicola
to her tent. She wondered if he would try to kiss her,
but he did not.

'Sleep well,' was all he said.

Nicola was getting ready for bed when she heard someone call her name.

She peered outside. 'Jason?'

'It's Lance. I want to talk to you, Nicola.'

'Lance! What are you doing here?'

'Come outside.'

'It's so late. Is something wrong?'

'Please,' he said.

'I'll be with you. Give me a moment.'

Nicola put on a heavy sweater, then she left the tent.
It was so dark that she could barely see Lance. But he
saw her. Taking her arm, he led her a little way from the
other tents, where they could talk without being
overheard.

'Why did you do it?' He flung the question at her.

'What. . . What did I do?' She stared up at him in confusion.

'Why did you sit with Jason at the fire?'

'You called me out just to ask me that?' she said disbelievingly.

'I need to know.'

'Couldn't it have waited till morning?'

'No. Why did you do it, Nicola?'

'He invited me to sit with him,' she said simply.

'You could have said no.'

'There was no reason to.'

'I was waiting for you. I'd saved you a space beside me.'

'We hadn't talked about it,' she said slowly.

'I took it for granted.'

This was ridiculous, Nicola thought, beginning to feel irritated. 'Maybe you shouldn't have done that,' she said, as pleasantly as she was able to in the circumstances. 'Look, Lance, I really didn't mean to hurt you.'

'But you did hurt me. You're *my* girl, not Jason's.'

'Lance. . .?' She looked at him, startled. Had Sally been right all along? 'I'm not your girl,' she said quietly. 'I never have been.'

'That's not true,' he said belligerently. 'Think of all the time we've spent together.'

'Because we're friends.' It was becoming difficult to speak calmly. 'Right from the start that's the way it's been. You found out I was Todd's sister, and you were his friend. You became my friend too.'

'I thought there was more to it.' His voice was flat and angry.

'I don't know why you should have. It's not as if I gave you any encouragement. And you. . .you've never

made any advances towards me, Lance. I didn't know it
was more than friendship on your part either.'

'Did you want me to paw you? Is that what you
wanted, Nicola?' he asked aggressively.

'Of course not!' She stepped closer to him and touched
his arm tentatively. 'You've been so kind to me, Lance,
and I'm so fond of you. Can't we just remain friends?'

He was silent for so long that Nicola began to wonder
if he meant to answer her at all. He was so close to her
that she could actually feel his tension.

At last he turned to her. 'I suppose we can be friends.'

'I'm glad, I really am. When we get back to Cape
Town you must spend some time with us. Todd will be
so thrilled with the photos, and I know he'll want to
thank you.'

After a moment, Lance said. 'Yes, well. . .'

A cool breeze swept the plateau and Nicola shivered.
'It's getting cold out here,' she said. 'Would you mind
very much if I left you now?'

'You want to go to bed. I won't delay you,' he said
brusquely. 'Goodnight.'

Nicola watched him vanish in the darkness, a rigid
angry man, fighting some inner demon which she did
not understand.

CHAPTER SEVEN

WHEN Nicola walked to the kitchen tent the next morning, the campsite was so deserted that she was certain she was the only person awake. And then she saw Jason, and remembered dreaming about him the previous night.

'Good morning,' he called as he came towards her.

'Hello, Jason.' She smiled at him as he stopped beside her. 'Been for a walk already?'

'Why do you ask?'

'Your hair is windblown, and your *veldskoene* are wet.'

'You *are* observant!'

His eyes sparkled as he grinned down at her, and Nicola felt a stirring inside her. It was not just that he was good-looking: he was so overwhelmingly vibrant and masculine, it would be impossible not to be moved by him.

'Actually,' he said, 'I've just got back. The rest of them don't know what they're missing when they toddle out of their sleeping-bags just in time for their pancakes.'

'You could show them.'

'I could show *you*.'

'Some time—that would be nice.'

'Now,' he said.

'You just reminded me that I have pancakes to make.'

'You could make them after our walk.'

'Then breakfast would be late, and you'd be able to fire me.' She threw him a sparkling look. 'Or is that the object of the exercise?'

'Is that what you think?'

'I only know that I'll never give you a chance to get rid of me. But you know that already.'

'*Never*?' he asked, holding her eyes.

She managed to hold the look, though it was difficult. 'Not for the duration of the trip.'

'I see,' he said. And then, 'How would it be if we walked together and I helped you with the breakfast after that?'

The suggestion was so unexpected, and so utterly and absolutely tempting, that Nicola's heart did a little somersault in her chest.

'The boss helping the cook?' she murmured.

'I think you've shown by now what you think of convention. Yes or no, Nicola?'

'Yes,' she said quickly.

Within minutes they were out of sight of the camp, walking along a trail that was so narrow that if she'd been alone Nicola might never have seen it. The underbrush was wet underfoot and against her jean-clad legs. Once they saw a startled *dassie* scampering through the wild grass, and though Nicola had seen many a rock rabbit on Table Mountain, she was nevertheless enchanted.

Higher went the path, and now there were little round stones underfoot which made climbing slippery. Without a word, Jason reached for Nicola's hand and drew her alongside him. The stones lasted only a little way, then there was greater traction once more, but Jason did not release her hand, and Nicola was content that it be so.

Now and then they stopped to look around them: at the brooding mountains, the strange rock formations, the coarse scrub and the trees that were bent permanently by the wind.

'It always fascinates me how the mountains change with the time of day,' said Nicola.

'Do you enjoy seeing them like this?'

'I *love* it! Reminds me of that first morning, when we walked together way down at the base camp. It's just a little wilder up here.'

'So then you're glad I persuaded you to come?'

'I wouldn't have missed it.'

Jason looked down at her, and there was an expression in his eyes that made her feel very excited. Also a little unnerved. There was something rather frightening about loving a man so much that all you wanted was to be in his arms.

'We're at a good echo point here,' he said then.

'Really?'

'Want to try it?'

'Could be fun,' she agreed.

'Hello!' he shouted.

Moments later the echo came answering back— hellooo!

It was Nicola's turn. 'Hello. . . Hello. . .'

Again the echo sounded, helloooo, hellooo—a little like Jason's, yet softer.

'Nicola!' Jason shouted.

Icolaaa! came the echo.

Nicola called, 'Jason!'

Ason! Ason! The echo bounded off the mountains around them.

And then they were both calling. Nicola! Jason! The echoes mingled, merged, a playful mixture that sounded like neither of their names, and yet, in an odd kind of way, like both of them.

At almost the same moment they ceased their shouting and looked at each other.

'Did you notice,' said Jason, 'the echoes we make are different?'

'But not unharmoniously so.' Her throat was dry now, though not from shouting.

'No.'

They looked at each other again, and then, at exactly the same moment, each took a step towards the other.

'We both know we're not really talking about echoes,' Jason said huskily.

'No,' Nicola said very softly, 'I know we aren't.'

'Do you think,' he asked, 'that it's possible for trust to be regained?'

'What do *you* think?'

'Until yesterday, when I saw you in a different way. . .with Linda. . .I might have said no.'

'And now?' Her throat had become so dry that it was difficult to speak.

'Maybe.' His eyes were troubled. 'You know how I feel about what you did. That I can't accept it.'

'Yes, I know.'

'And yet. . . You're so lovely, Nicola. So beautiful and sexy and desirable. So filled with courage and independence and drive. When I met you I knew I'd never. . .'

He stopped and put his arms around her and drew her against him. Her mouth was against his throat, his pulse beat against her lips. She felt his lips moving in her hair.

At length he lifted his head. 'Maybe what we need is time,' he said.

'We have time.' For the first time in days she let herself hope.

'Look at me, Nicola.'

She looked up at him, and with something like pain in his voice, he said, 'Why did you have to be so damned beautiful? I go mad every time I see you. Every time I think of you.'

'I didn't know that,' she whispered.

'Didn't you? I dream about you at night, I ache for you during the day. I want you so much.'

'I'm here,' she said softly.

'Nicola. . .'

She heard the rough sound in his throat the moment before he bent his head towards hers. And then he was kissing her, his mouth urgent, his tongue pushing at her lips. The force of his passion brought a moan of pleasure surging up through Nicola's throat. Her slim body arched itself against his, convulsed by a longing that was like nothing she had ever known.

Briefly Jason lifted his head, and they looked into each other's eyes. They began to touch each other's faces, learning, exploring planes and valleys and textures. Jason's hand went beneath the heavy fall of Nicola's hair, sliding around towards the front of her throat, brushing it, his fingers feather-light on all the most sensitive places. Nicola caressed his cheeks, his eyes, his eyelids, until suddenly her hands went behind his head and buried themselves in the thick dark hair at the nape of his neck.

And then they were kissing again—passionately, rapturously, as if they could never get enough of each other. Jason's hands went to Nicola's hips. As he drew her against him she felt the throbbing hardness of his body, and she was filled with an immense happiness at the knowledge of how much he wanted her.

For she wanted him too. Oh, how she wanted him! She was a virgin, yet making love with this man held no fears for her. She felt as if she were drowning in a sea of touch and sensation in which the only reality was Jason and the pleasure they were able to give each other.

'We have to find a place to go,' Jason said at length. 'That secret place we once talked about. Remember?'

'Yes. . .'

'There's no privacy at the camp.'

The camp. Sanity returned, though slowly. 'We should be getting back,' Nicola said breathlessly.

'No!'

'You know we do.'

'All I know is that we need a place,' Jason murmured, moving her hips against his.

'I know. . .' Her sanity was threatening to desert her once more.

'But if we have to get back, then let's go now,' he said. 'Beore there's no going back for either of us.'

They reached the camp and found that the first people were beginning to stir. Craig gave them a sleepy look as he walked by with his shaving kit in his hand and a towel slung across his shoulder. Martha Baynes peered out of her tent, glanced up at the mountains, rubbed her eyes, then vanished from view again. They heard her calling to her husband, telling him it was going to be a good day and to get out of his sleeping-bag if he wanted some breakfast.

Jason was as good as his word. He went with Nicola to the kitchen tent, and while she began to make the pancake batter he started on the sandwiches for the picnic lunches. By the time everyone in the group was dressed and ready to eat, the coffee was made, the long trestle-tables had been laid, the pancakes were warm and golden, and the lunches had been packed.

'I'd say we made good progress,' said Jason, turning to Nicola with a smile.

'Excellent progress,' she agreed.

'In more than one sense?'

She nodded, unable to speak. She had a feeling that her heart was in her eyes when she looked at him.

There were other things Jason had to do then: there

were group leaders to talk to, details to discuss. He swallowed a pancake and a mug of coffee and walked out of the kitchen tent. Nicola watched him go, and wondered when she had felt quite so happy.

Breakfast was over and she was starting to clear up, when Lance walked over to her for the first time that morning.

'Nicola. . .?'

She turned. 'Why, Lance!'

He was looking at her feet. 'Your shoes are wet and there's grass all over them. Have you been somewhere?'

'I was out walking.'

'By yourself?'

'With Jason,' she said quietly, trying not to show her irritation.

He was silent a moment, his expression tight and hard. And then, quite suddenly, all his anger seemed to leave him. 'I'm sorry,' he said. 'I shouldn't have asked.'

Nicola looked at him in astonishment. After last night this sudden about-face was not what she had expected. 'There's nothing wrong with a walk, Lance,' she said quietly.

'Of course not, you're quite right, there's nothing at all wrong with it. That's it, Nicola. I want to apologise. I behaved very badly yesterday.'

'It's OK. Don't think about it.'

'But I shouldn't have done it. You must have felt I was pushing you.'

'You were pushing a bit, but why don't we just put it behind us now?' she said generously.

'I'd like that. I'm sorry about what happened, Nicola. Really I am. I feel very strongly about you, and I suppose. . . Well, I hoped you felt the same way about me.'

'Lance, please. . .'

'What I'm saying is. . .I must have misunderstood. And I'm sorry.'

'I'm sorry too, Lance. I never intended to mislead you. I didn't think I had. And I really did mean what I said about being friends.'

'It's less than I wanted. But I'll try and settle for it—for now.'

'You really are nice,' she said warmly.

'Is that what you say to Jason?'

'*Lance*!'

'Sorry. *Sorry*! I shouldn't have said that either. It's just that I get the feeling that you and Jason——'

'Don't go on with this,' she pleaded. 'Please, don't go on with it.'

'I won't, I promise. Listen, Nicola, I have this fantastic hike planned for today. You are coming out with me, aren't you?'

'I'm not sure,' she hedged.

Jason was going with one of the other groups, she knew. They were off to a cave to look at rock paintings, and there was a part of her that yearned to go with them.

'Please come. You'll see plants you didn't see lower down. And it's going to be a perfect day for photos. Will you, Nicola?'

Lance was looking at her with a pleading, crooked, boyish smile that was hard to resist. Smiling back at him, she said, 'I'd like that very much.'

Lance had been right. There were plants along the trail that Nicola had not seen until now. She shot a whole spool of film within the first two hours of the hike, and in her notebook she jotted down all the names and details which Lance gave her with such eagerness.

He must be every bit as much an expert as Todd, she

thought. With so much in common, it was no wonder the two had been friends.

'Do you think we'll find the purple aloe?' she asked him.

'I'm not sure.'

'Todd says it's there, beyond the bridge somewhere.'

'Maybe. . .'

'But you don't really think so?'

'I'm sceptical,' Lance admitted. 'I've never quite believed in that particular aloe myself.'

'But we might find it.'

'"Might" being the key word, Nicola.'

'I'm keeping a whole spool in reserve in case we do.'

'Don't get your hopes up too high,' he said, but gently.

On the trail, there was no hint of the haunted man Nicola had seen the previous day and this morning. Lance was relaxed and friendly. He even cracked a few jokes, which was unusual for him.

True, now and then, if Nicola happened to turn his way unexpectedly, she'd find him watching her with a kind of odd intensity. But he did not utter another jealous or possessive word. And the moment he caught her looking at him, his expression would soften as his lips curved in a quick smile.

It was just after midday when Nicola saw the men. She heard their singing even before she saw them—the rhythmic chanting of workmen raising their picks to the beat of their song. Though they were at least half a mile further up the cliffside, the sound they made carried easily on the still air.

'Look, Lance!' Nicola cried. 'There are people up there.'

'Quarry workers.'

'We can go up and talk to them.'

'Why would you want to do that?'

'They might know something. About the bridge. About Todd.'

Lance looked at her a moment. Then he said, 'We're not going that way. Our path is much lower.'

'I know, but there's another path. I can see it—it cuts across to the top one. Lance, please!'

'It wouldn't be fair to the others. It's barren, no vegetation. There's nothing of interest up there.'

'But, Lance——'

'What do you think those men can tell you, Nicola? They spend all their time at the quarry. They're miles away from the bridge.'

'They might just know *something*,' she insisted.

'They don't. They can't.'

'Nevertheless, I have to speak to them. So far all I've done since we got here is take photos. I need to find out about the bridge.'

'You know what happened,' he said. He was beginning to sound impatient.

'No!'

'In any event, we're not going that way. Just look at the climb it would be. I'm sorry, but it would be irresponsible of me to ask the rest of the group to attempt it.'

They walked further, into a patch of cacti—unusual specimens which they had seen nowhere else. Lance tried to persuade Nicola to photograph them.

But Nicola had no eyes for the cacti. Now she could think only of the quarry workers.

They were halfway back to camp when she said to Lance, 'I can see why you didn't want to ask the group to do the climb up to the quarry.'

He shot her a quick smile. 'I knew you'd understand.'

'But couldn't *we* go? You and I?'

'And leave the others to go back alone?'

'It's not a difficult trail from here. They'd find their way back easily.'

'No, Nicola, I'm sorry.'

'Later, then?'

'It really isn't possible.'

'I have to speak to them. Don't you see?'

'I see that you're becoming obsessed with those men,' he said. 'Look, Nicola, if there was even the slightest chance—the very slightest—that they could tell us something, I'd do it. You know that I'm every bit as distressed about what happened at the bridge as you are. But they don't know anything. There's no way they could.'

Nicola was silent a few minutes. Then she said, 'Perhaps Jason would go with me.'

'Forget it! All that way up the mountainside on a wild-goose chase? You don't know him at all if you think he'd do that.'

'In that case, maybe I should just go on my own.'

'*Nicola*! I don't believe you said that.'

'It's just a thought, Lance,' she said quietly.

'One you'd better push right out of your mind. Jason would never allow it. Neither would I, for that matter.'

His tone was so vehement that there was obviously no point in going on with it. But if Lance had definite ideas on the matter of the quarrymen, so did Nicola. They were the first people—other than the members of the tour—whom Nicola had seen since coming on the trip. She knew she had to speak to them.

There was no sign of Jason when they got back to camp. Nicola was not surprised, for the bushmen paintings were quite a distance away. It would be some time before that particular group returned.

She washed and changed into other clothes, then she

went to the kitchen tent. Curry tonight, she decided. It would make a nice change from the simple *braaivleis* of the previous day. Only for the Bayneses would she make something different, for Martha had told her that she and Henry did not enjoy spicy food. *Sosaties*, she decided, remembering that Henry had had three helpings the last time.

For the next half-hour she chopped and mixed and tasted. Hearing some of the other groups return to camp, she popped her head out of the tent, but Jason was not in sight. Linda was there, though, and she joined Nicola and insisted on helping her.

Not until supper did Nicola see Jason. Plate in hand, he came to compliment her on the curry.

'Delicious,' he said. 'I hope you make this again.'

'Now that I know it's appreciated, it will be my pleasure.'

'It was nice of you to make something different for Martha and Henry,' Jason added.

She smiled at him. 'Most people I know seem to love curry, yet Todd choked on it the last time I made it for him.'

'He didn't!'

'He did—but I think I overdid the spices that day.'

'That would explain it.' He was smiling too, the smile that found its way into her dreams every night.

And then he said, 'Talking of Todd, Lance told me about the quarrymen.'

'*He did*?' she echoed.

'He seemed to think you might try going up to the quarry alone.'

'Lance actually made a point of telling you that?'

'Don't look so surprised, Nicola, Lance isn't a school-boy telling tales.'

Strangely, Nicola felt as if Lance had done exactly that.

'Is it true, Nicola?' Jason persisted.

'The thought did cross my mind,' she admitted.

'I want you to forget it.'

'But I'd really like to talk to the men, Jason.'

'You'd be wasting your time. They never go near the bridge, there's nothing they could tell you.'

'That's what Lance said. But I feel I owe it to Todd to try, all the same.'

'You know what happened at the bridge, Nicola.'

'You keep saying that, yet you know I don't believe it.'

'You really are a stubborn woman! Maybe that's another reason I find you so attractive.' He sounded part humorous, part exasperated. 'The fact is, tomorrow is our last day at this site, and there are other hikes planned. Nobody is going anywhere near the quarry.'

'You don't think it's possible one of the groups could go that way?'

'There's nothing up there except dust and grit. Nobody would hike that way for fun.'

'Would you come with me?' She looked at him pleadingly.

He laughed. 'You know I find it hard to resist you, so would you please stop looking at me like that?'

'Will you, Jason?'

'I can't,' he said. 'I have to check on one of the other trails tomorrow, and I'll be away most of the day. I'm sorry, Nicola.'

'I'm sorry too. . .'

It made no sense that Nicola should feel there was a conspiracy afoot to keep her from the quarry. But there it was, she was beginning to feel that way.

Jason looked down at her. 'I take it Lance *was* mistaken? You wouldn't go up there alone?'

'Would it be so wrong?' she asked.

'Absolutely. It's a long, lonely path, and they're a rough lot up there at the quarry. I won't have you—or any of the other women—going up there alone.'

'You really are concerned,' she said thoughtfully.

'Because it's not safe.'

'What could possibly happen?'

'Anything. You could fall, and nobody would ever know. Worse still, you could be assaulted.'

'I think you're exaggerating!' she laughed.

'I am not. Listen to me, Nicola, I absolutely forbid you to go up there.'

'*Forbid*? That's a strong word to use to an adult woman.'

'Maybe it is, but I'm concerned about your safety. Do I have your word that you won't go up to the quarry?'

Nicola looked at him, and suddenly she smiled. 'I think we're both making too much of nothing. At this particular moment I have no plans to go anywhere. So how about another helping of curry?'

'Sounds good to me,' he said. 'And after that I'll help you clean up, so you can get finished quickly and sit beside me at the camp-fire.'

Next morning Nicola joined Lance's group again. She had thought of joining one of the other groups for a change, but decided against it when she realised that none of them were going anywhere near the quarry. The thought of staying in the camp for the day had crossed her mind too—she could wash her hair and read—but she still had the hope that Lance might relent and lead the hike in the direction she wanted.

Once more her hopes came to nothing. Now and then

during the morning she saw glimpses of the quarry—a puff of dust, the blade of a pick glinting in the sun, a cart of some kind being trundled around. She even heard the sound of the workers' rhythmic singing. But that was as close as she came to the place where she so badly wanted to be. A feeling of depression began to come over her.

For once they returned to the camp at noon. Lance had planned two short hikes for the day rather than one long one. The afternoon trail would take them in a different direction altogether, he told Nicola when she asked.

Her mind was made up in an instant. After lunch, when Lance said he was ready to set out once more, Nicola told him she'd decided to stay behind.

'Why?' he asked.

'I've things to do.'

'What things?' His eyes were suspicious.

'Come on, Lance!' She threw him a teasing grin. 'You don't really want to know about all the things that keep a girl busy. Stop worrying about me—I won't be bored.'

'Well, all right,' he said. But he did not look at all happy.

As soon as Lance and the others were out of sight, Nicola left the camp. The sense of oppression that had been with her all morning lifted as she began to walk. She had begun to feel as if she might never find out what she needed to know. Now at last, *at last*, she was doing something constructive to help her brother. The afternoon's mission could well be futile; the men at the quarry might know nothing. But if she did not speak to them she would always wonder if there had been something they could have told her.

As Jason had warned, the path up the mountainside

was long and winding. Dust, thick and dry and kicked
up by her shoes, clogged her nostrils, loose stones rolled
beneath her feet as she walked. On either side of the
path the earth was arid. If there had been vegetation
here once, the quarry dust had killed it off long ago.

More than anything, the path was steep, so that Nicola
found her progress much slower than she had antici-
pated. The quarry had seemed quite near when she'd
looked at it from the hiking trail, yet it was more than
an hour before she reached it.

The rhythmic chanting ceased abruptly the moment
the men saw her. Eyes peered at her curiously from
dusty faces. Nobody said a word. At length one man,
evidently the foreman, stepped forward.

'Good afternoon.' Nicola gave him her warmest smile.
'I'm sorry I interrupted the work.'

'Afternoon, lady. You from the camp?'

'Yes.'

'Are you lost?'

'No. I came up here because I wanted to speak to
you.'

His response to that was a baffled look.

Nicola glanced around her. 'Is there somewhere we
can talk?'

He pointed. 'Up there. . .'

He led her towards a cluster of tents and corrugated
iron shacks. On one side was a three-sided canvas
awning. In the shade beneath the canvas were a few
camp-stools, a Primus stove, some mugs and an open
packet of tea.

The foreman made a gesture towards one of the dusty
camp-stools. Nicola hesitated just a moment, the sat
down. The man did not sit, but stood looking down at her.

'What can I do for you, lady?' he asked.

'There was an accident,' Nicola said, coming straight

to the point. 'A few months ago. A bridge collapsed. I think it was just a few miles from here.'

'I heard about it,' said the man.

'Do you know anything about it?'

'Fraid not.'

'Nothing at all?'

'No, ma'am. We never have any business at the bridge. Never go further than the quarry.'

So Jason and Lance had been right after all. Nicola tried to hide her disappointment. 'The other men. . . Is it possible one of them might know something?'

'No, lady, I'm sure they don't.'

'Well,' she said, 'thanks anyway. I was here, and I thought I'd try. I suppose I'd best be going now.'

The man nodded and went back to join the other workers. In minutes the chanting and the sound of metal striking rock had resumed once again.

Nicola started to walk. At the edge of the quarry she stopped. Far below her she could see the camp. It was going to be a long way down.

She had not gone far when footsteps sounded behind her, and, turning, she saw the foreman coming towards her.

'I just remembered,' he said. 'There is a man you can talk to.'

'*Who?*'

'A prospector—weird old fellow. His name is Herman Tyler.'

'Do you think he might know something about the accident?'

'Couldn't say, lady, I really don't know.'

'Where can I find him?' asked Nicola.

'He lives in a shack by the bridge.'

'He lives by the bridge?' she echoed.

'That's what made me think of him.'

'I'll make sure I speak to him.' Nicola's eyes shone.

'If he'll speak to you, lady. Doesn't like strangers, old Herman doesn't. As for that tour of yours, he hates it. He's unsociable-like.'

'I'll do my very best to speak to him all the same,' Nicola said. 'You don't know how you've helped me. Thank you so much!'

She had made progress! Somewhere near the bridge there was a man called Herman Tyler, and she would talk to him. Filled with excitement, Nicola began the descent down the mountain path. It would not take her long, for going downhill had to be a lot easier than climbing. She would be back at camp before anyone had a chance to miss her.

It wasn't long before she found that going downhill could be more difficult than going up. The downward slope was so steep as to make walking difficult. Nicola found that she had to keep straining her body backwards to keep from falling. Stones slithered beneath her feet, and once or twice she felt her feet sliding on the uneven surface. The strain of holding her body in check made her thigh and calf muscles ache. Twice she slipped, but each time she managed to break the fall with her hands.

She was negotiating a steep cluster of rocks when a sudden rush of air above her head made her look up. Just a few feet above her head was a bird, a huge bird with a cruelly curved beak and a strong wing-span. At the very moment that Nicola looked up, the bird made a sudden downward swoop. Instinctively, she shrank back. The abruptness of the movement broke her balance, and a moment later she lay sprawled sideways on the rough stone.

The bird soared and swooped, then soared again before wheeling away towards an adjacent cliff.

Nicola began to stand, only to find that a searing pain in her right ankle caused her to sink back on to the rock. A minute passed and the pain subsided. Once more she made the effort to stand, and once more her right foot buckled beneath her.

Darn it! She turned her head and looked upwards, the way she had come. Had anyone seen her fall? The quarry was out of sight, but perhaps someone would come to her aid.

Nothing stirred on the dusty path above her.

'Help!' she shouted, trying to aim her voice in the direction of the quarry. 'Help! Help!'

The sound of singing drifted towards her through the silent air. Would the men hear her?

'Help!' she called again and again, until her throat was raw.

But the rhythm of the song and the sound of the picks on the stone never altered. And the echoes sent out by the quarrymen drowned the echoes of her calls.

What on earth was she going to do? Two hours from now it would be dark. She could not spend the night alone, without even a sweater, on the bare mountainside.

Someone would miss her—Sally perhaps, when she went to the tent to change into warm clothes; or the rest of them when they discovered that there was no supper. They would look for her in the camp, and eventually they would send out a search party. But by then it would be too dark to see. And besides, she had told nobody where she was going.

There was nothing for it—she would have to make her way on all fours. It would take her an age to get down, but anything was better than staying up here in this dreadful spot while she waited for help that might not come that night.

Inch by anguished inch, she started down the dusty

path. In rocky places, she slid on her rear from one rock to another, using her hands to lever herself along. Where pebbles and underbrush covered the path, she found it easier to crawl. The going was painful. In no time at all her knees felt raw; they were beginning to bleed. But she could not let that hold her back. Sally would clean her up with water and soap and disinfectant when she got back to camp. Her priority now was to get there.

Now and then she looked at her watch, and was horrified to see how much time had passed since her fall and how little ground she had covered since then. She tried to quicken her pace, but there was a limit to how quickly she could move. It would be dark long before she covered a quarter of the way. She would not—*could not*—let herself wonder what she would do when she could no longer see where she was going. She would have to go on anyway.

After a while she stopped looking at her watch. Seeing how quickly the minutes passed only made her panic. She began to lose all sense of time, the only measure that meant anything became the distance she was able to cover.

At first, when she heard the sound, it did not register on her weary mind. Again it came, and again, until suddenly she did hear it.

'Nicola. . . Nicola!' And then the echo: 'Icolaa. . . Icolaa!'

'*Here*! I'm here!' she cried.

'Nicola. . . Nicola!'

'Help! Help!' she called back.

It was another ten minutes before Jason came striding around a bend in the trail. Dizzy with relief, Nicola held out her arms to him.

'You found me! Oh, Jason, I should have known you would!'

'No thanks to you!' he snapped.

CHAPTER EIGHT

NICOLA was shocked when Jason made no effort to kneel and take her in his arms. She was even more shocked when she registered the expression of utter fury in his face. For the first time she realised quite how angry he had sounded.

'You did come looking for me?' she said tentatively.

'It's hardly coincidence that I chose to walk along this hellish trail. Though on second thoughts, maybe I should have left you here for the night.'

'Jason! I don't believe you're talking to me like this!' she gasped.

'Believe it,' he said abruptly.

'You're so angry.'

'Angrier than I'd have believed possible.'

'Can't you see that I've fallen?'

'I'm not blind, Nicola. Nor am I insensitive. I also remember telling you that this could happen.'

'I know, but I thought. . . I didn't think you would mind when you realised that I——'

'Save the excuses for later,' Jason bit out curtly. 'Right now I'm in no mood to hear them. Can you stand up?'

'No. And I can't walk,' she said, her tone subdued.

'Why not?'

'I slipped on some rocks. . .further up. . . There was this bird, you see. I think it was an eagle, and it came so close that it frightened me. Anyway, I fell.'

Something moved in his eyes. For a moment she saw what might have been the glimmer of compassion in his expression. But when he spoke the curtness was still in his tone.

'Have you broken anything?' he asked.

'I don't think so. But I'm all cut up, and I think I might have sprained my ankle quite badly.'

'I'll carry you,' he said.

'All the way?' she asked doubtfully. 'Won't I be too heavy for you? Perhaps you should go back for some help.'

'There's no time for that. I have to get you off this path before dark.'

He managed to carry her all the way. It was an agonising journey. Mostly he carried her on his back, piggy-back style. He did not complain once that her weight was too much for him, but she knew he was under great pressure. Beneath her body she could feel his muscles, hard as the rock on which she'd fallen. The back of his throat was corded with strain, and his shirt was wet with sweat.

Nicola's ankle throbbed with pain, but she would not have told Jason so even if he had asked her. In fact, not a single word passed between. Once, when he put her down so that he could rest his weary back, she opened her mouth to say something, but the look he threw her was so ominous that she left the remark unsaid.

It was dark by the time they reached the camp. People gathered, their faces curious at the sight of Nicola on Jason's back. But a look at Jason's face, and the questions stopped on their lips.

Lance came towards them. 'What happened? Nicola, are you hurt? Jason, are you OK? Why didn't you call for help?'

Jason walked past him without answering. Nicola remained silent as well.

In the nursing tent, Jason stopped, let Nicola slide to

the ground, and turned to Sally. 'Patient for you. Take
a look at her, please, will you? Apart from anything else,
her hands and knees will need a decent scrubbing.'

'Oh, lord!' Sally was wide-eyed as she looked at
Nicola.

'Let me know when you've finished,' said Jason.
'Then I'll take her back to her tent.'

It took Sally quite a while to wash the grit from Nicola's
knees. She worked slowly and very gently, pausing now
and then to let Nicola catch her breath. Yet, gentle as
Sally was, the process was so painful that Nicola's
muscles were stiff with tension and she had to bite her
lips hard to stop herself from crying.

'That bad?' asked Sally, her eyes warm with concern.

''Fraid so. . .'

'You can cry, I don't mind.'

'I don't want to.'

'Poor Nicola, I'm sorry I have to hurt you, but you've
collected so much dirt in your skin. . .'

'I know. Don't think I don't appreciate what you're
doing.' Nicola stopped once more to catch her breath.
Then she asked, 'Sal, was it you who sent Jason to find
me? When did you realise I was missing?'

Sally carefully removed a tiny pebble from Nicola's
knee before she answered. 'Actually, you have Lance to
thank for that.'

'*Lance?*'

'He was looking for you. Apparently he'd just returned
from a hike. He was quite concerned when he couldn't
find you, and he spoke to Jason.'

'So it was Lance. I thought maybe. . .'

'At first everyone thought he was making a great fuss
about nothing, that you had to be somewhere around the
camp. But after a while, when you didn't show up, we

all started wondering where you could be. That's when Lance remembered that you'd been so keen to go up to the quarry. He had a hunch you might have gone up there on your own. I believe he was about to start looking for you, but Jason insisted on going himself.'

'And now Jason is furious with me.'

'So I gathered.' Sally gave her another compassionate look.

'I had to go to the quarry, Sal,' Nicola said earnestly. 'I really did have to go.'

'I know.'

'I can understand Jason being a bit angry. But not quite *so* angry.'

'He was worried. He'll get over it.'

'I wonder. . .'

'Here, the knees are all bandaged, now let me take a look at your ankle,' Sally said. 'My goodness, Nicola, you gave it quite a sprain, didn't you? You won't be walking on this for a while.'

'About Jason. . .' Nicola's mind was not on her ankle at that moment.

'He never stays angry for long,' her friend said cheerfully. 'He'll be over it by the time you see him.'

But when Jason appeared a while later, he looked far from being over it. He looked down at Nicola, and listened quietly while Sally told him about the sprain, and all the while his expression never changed. It was as if he had drawn a mask over his face. A tight mask of anger and contempt.

After thanking Sally for her help, he bent, lifted Nicola into his arms and carried her out of the nursing tent. He had washed and changed his clothes. His arms and throat felt cool against her skin, and his body had a clean masculine smell that filled her with a familiar longing.

Nicola yearned to put her arm around his neck, but she knew that even the slightest intimacy at this moment would bring forth an outburst of scorn that she would not know how to cope with.

He carried her to her tent and put her down on her sleeping-bag. Gratefully, Nicola lay back—only to sit up in alarm a moment later.

'Supper,' she said. 'I have to go and see about it.'

'Don't be ridiculous! You're in no state to see about anything.'

'People will be starving,' she protested.

'Thanks to Linda, they will not. The moment she saw me carry you into the camp she insisted on filling your place.'

His manner was icy. Sally had been wrong. Jason showed not the slightest hint of softening.

'You have your wish,' she said slowly.

'Meaning?'

'I've given you reason to fire me.'

'Believe me,' he said, 'I've never been more tempted. If we weren't so far away from civilisation at this point, I'd send you packing at daylight.'

'I think you really would. Jason, you're so terribly angry. Don't you realise, if I hadn't fallen none of this would have happened?'

'You didn't have to fall, Nicola. You didn't have to be on that wretched trail in the first place.'

'I had to go to the quarry,' she insisted.

'Even after I made it quite clear that I didn't want you to go there!'

'Todd. . . His reputation. . . His chances of ever making something really good of his book, of getting a university post. I had to ask the quarrymen if they knew anything. Don't you understand?'

'I understand,' he said, 'that you lied to me.'

'I *lied*?' She looked at him, shocked. 'I didn't lie to you!'

'Yes, Nicola, you did. You knew how strongly I felt about that first pack of lies. And then you did it again.'

'But I didn't lie.'

'I forbade you to go to the quarry.'

'I remember telling you it was a strong word to use.'

'And I remember asking you if Lance was right—if you still planned to go. I also remember your answer, Nicola. You said that at that moment you had no plans to go anywhere.'

'That was true! I didn't have any plans—not then.'

'Maybe nothing definite, but you were thinking about it. So your answer was just a way of changing the subject, of putting me off.'

'I never said I was *not* going to the quarry,' Nicola insisted.

'You certainly didn't say you *were* going. Or even that you were seriously considering it.'

'Was that really so bad?'

'You were dishonest by omission, Nicola. You knew how I felt, but you were determined to go anyway. You kept quiet about your plans. You probably figured I'd never know. And if you hadn't got stranded you might have been right.'

'That's not quite the way it was, Jason.'

'It's the way I see it.'

'I didn't plan it the way you seem to think. In fact, when I did go up the mountain it was on impulse.' She stopped and looked at him, and saw that he was not convinced. 'Don't you see, I was desperate. The last day at this site, and my only chance to——'

She stopped as she saw that he was about to leave the tent. 'You don't really want to hear about it, do you?'

'No,' Jason said deliberately, 'I do not. You and Todd

have a lot in common. On the surface you're such a charismatic pair. It's so hard not to like you. Beneath it all, you're single-minded and stubborn and relentless.'

'You make us sound so awful!' she sighed.

'I'm just telling you how I see you. You and Todd both behave the same way, Nicola. You stop at nothing to get what you want. And if anyone is hurt or inconvenienced in the process—well, that's just too bloody bad, isn't it?'

'That's not fair,' Nicola protested, feeling a little ill.

'I'm not talking fairness. I'm telling you that I've had about as much as I can take of you and your precious brother!' With which words he walked out of the tent.

Nicola spent a restless night. The argument with Jason had upset her very much, for she knew now that he would never trust her again.

She woke the next morning, wondering how she was going to cope with the things she had to do that day. That issue, at least, was one that need not have concerned her. Sally helped her out of her sleeping-bag, then helped her to get dressed. Walking was going to be a problem, for the ankle was still so painful that Nicola could not put any weight on it.

She'd hooked her arm through Sally's and was about to hobble out of the tent, when Lance appeared. Ignoring her protests, he insisted on carrying her to the kitchen tent, where he placed her very gently on a chair beside the big trestle-table where she did all her food preparation.

'Thanks,' she said gratefully. 'That was kind of you.'

'It's the least I could do,' he said. 'I feel so bad about what happened yesterday.'

'No reason why *you* should feel bad,' she said.

'But there is. I knew you wanted to go the quarry, but

I still didn't realise quite how much it meant to you. If I had, I would have skipped the hike and taken you there myself.'

'I could still have fallen.'

'But Jason would never have known.' He hesitated a moment. 'I believe he was angry?'

'That's putting it mildly,' Nicola said unhappily. 'I'd rather not talk about that, if you don't mind.'

'I understand,' he said comfortingly. 'But I'm curious about one thing—did you achieve anything at the quarry?'

'*Yes*! Just listen to this, Lance! I was given a name. Did you know that there's a man who lives by the bridge?'

Lance frowned. 'Nobody lives up there, Nicola.'

'According to the foreman, someone does. A prospector, a man by the name of Tyler. Herman Tyler.'

'Obviously the foreman has his facts wrong. There's nobody up there.'

'You don't seem at all pleased with my news,' Nicola said, surprised. 'This man might know something. He might have seen something. Just think what it would mean to Todd if he did!'

In an instant Lance's expression had cleared. 'Of course I'm pleased. At least, I would be if I thought there was something in what you're saying. It would be wonderful if we could find out something that would clear Todd's name.'

'Yes, it would.'

'If I didn't seem enthusiastic—it's just that I don't want you to get your hopes up. Maybe there was a man once, but he probably moved away long ago. If there was anyone up there, don't you think we'd have seen him?'

'Maybe not. The foreman said he was a bit of a loner.'

'Look, Nicola. . . I know how much all this means to you. It's just. . . I think you're getting a bit too excited.'

'Maybe. And maybe you're right, and there's nobody there any more. On the other hand, there *could* be. I intend to make every effort I can to find this Herman Tyler. If he's not there, at least I'll know I tried.'

'I guess you're right. . .'

Nicola glanced at her watch. 'My goodness, look at the time! I have to get moving if I don't want to be late with the breakfast and the lunches.'

To her surprise, Lance insisted on helping her. A few minutes later Linda and Sally walked into the tent together, and announced that they had come to help her too.

'You helped me when I fell,' Linda said, when Nicola tried to thank her for all she was doing for her. 'The very least I can do is help you now that you're in trouble.'

Another surprise helper arrived in the form of Graham, the anthropologist. He and Linda seemed to be spending more and more time together. Nicola shot Linda a glance and saw the sparkle in her friend's eyes.

In no time they were sharing the various tasks between them. Lance and Graham carried the crockery and cutlery outside and began to lay the long picnic tables. Sally and Linda made the breakfast. Still sitting in her chair, Nicola got on with the lunch sandwiches.

Only of Jason there was no sign. Obviously he thought that Nicola would find a way of coping with her chores.

Shortly after breakfast, they packed up the camp and moved on. Lance helped Nicola on to her horse, and Sally secured the sprained ankle in a way that would give her the least pain.

They had just started out on the trail when Jason rode up beside her.

'Ankle hurting, Nicola?' His eyes were so impersonal that she wondered why he bothered to ask.

'A little.'

'Will you be all right?'

'Oh, yes. I think so.'

He hesitated, then he said, 'We can still turn back at this point. If you're in a lot of pain, we could delay the move by a day.'

'Don't even consider it,' she said, hiding her surprise at his suggestion. 'I'll manage. I'll find a way of managing.'

'One thing you've never lacked is guts, Nicola.'

She looked round at him then, and caught something moving in his eyes. Warmth? Admiration? Whatever it was, it was gone so quickly that she could not be sure.

A little unsteadily, she said, 'Jason. . .'

'Sally has pain-killers if you need them.'

It was not what she'd wanted him to say, and she knew that he knew it. 'Your concern surprises me,' she said bitterly.

'It shouldn't,' he said. 'You have certain qualities I don't care for, but that doesn't mean I wish you pain. I'm not an ogre, Nicola.'

His eyes swept her so impersonally that she knew she must have imagined seeing any warmth in them moments ago. 'In case you're wondering,' he said, 'I would show the same consideration to any other member of this group.'

The ride to the next campsite took the best part of the day. There were many times when Nicola's ankle ached, when she wished she had in fact taken Jason up on his suggestion. But after his last hateful remarks she would not have given him the satisfaction of telling him how she felt, or asking him to turn back.

As it was, she was never alone. Sally, guessing what she was going through, made sure that she took pain-killers regularly. Linda did whatever she could to help. When they stopped for a break she and Sally insisted on doing all the things that Nicola would normally have done. It was Linda who poured the coffee, while Sally handed out the picnic lunches. Between them, they made sure that everyone had what they needed.

As for Lance, he was at Nicola's side almost constantly. Ten times in two hours he asked her how she was feeling, whether he should ask Sally for more pain-killers. When they stopped for lunch he helped Nicola off her horse, and back on again later. His concern for her seemed to have no limits.

It was late in the afternoon when they arrived at the new campsite. Higher and even more remote than the last one had been, this was their last stopping place before they rode to the site near the bridge.

A few members of staff had ridden on ahead of the others, so that by the time the rest of the group arrived most of the tents were already set up. Nicola's ankle was throbbing badly now, and she wanted nothing more than to crawl into her sleeping-bag for a while. At the same time the excitement of being in this place gripped her.

Holding on to Lance's arm, she managed to hobble to a viewpoint a little way from the tents.

'Where's the bridge?' she asked.

'Still quite a way from here, Nicola.'

'Which direction?'

'Up there.' Lance made a vague gesture upwards and to the right.

'And somewhere up there there may be a man called Herman Tyler, and I'm going to talk to him.'

'What about your foot?'

'My ankle will be healed by the time we get to the bridge.'

'Maybe. . .'

'Even if it isn't. I'll make sure I don't let it get in my way.'

She turned, and found that Lance was looking at her, not at the view.

'You think I'm a little crazy, don't you?' she asked.

'Crazy? No.' His eyes were bright and hard and intense. 'You see, I know how you feel, Nicola.'

'You do?'

'When something is more important to you than anything else in the world, you let nothing stand in the way of your getting it.'

Nicola stared at him. 'The way you said that. . . It's as if there was something terribly important in your own life at this very moment.'

A quick smile chased the intensity from his eyes. 'Heavens no! My own life couldn't be more uncomplicated. I was just making a general observation. Come along, Nicola, you've been standing on that foot long enough. Time to get back.'

With Lance's help, Nicola hobbled to the kitchen tent. She was not surprised when Linda and Sally arrived minutes later to prepare for the evening *braaivleis*. By the time it was dark and the fires had been lit, the meat had been laid out, the potatoes were parboiled and wrapped in foil, and the salads were ready.

There was even more excitement than usual on this first night in a new place, for this was the spot from which they would leave, a few days from now, on a two-day expedition. For once, the group would hike together in one cohesive unit. The camp would remain the base where they would leave their belongings and to which they would return, but they would spend two nights away from it.

Nicola had heard so much from Todd about this expedition. She was looking forward to it as much as everyone else.

Sally was pleased with the way the sprained ankle was healing, but whenever Nicola asked the anxious question, 'Do you think I'll manage the expedition?' Sally's answer was always the same.

'We'll have to judge it closer to the time.'

'I've been waiting for this!' Nicola said excitedly, when Sally removed the last bandage the day before the expedition was due to set out.

'It's healed really well.' Sally sounded pleased.

'Fantastic! I was concerned I might not be able to go with the rest of you.'

'Nicola. . . Although your ankle has healed, it's still quite fragile,' Sally warned.

'It will be fine.'

'I'm not sure you should go on the expedition. It might be a bit much for you.'

'Sal, what are you saying! Of course I'm going.'

'You're going nowhere,' said a stern voice from the entrance of the nursing tent.

Nicola wheeled. 'You've been listening!' she accused Jason.

'I was coming in to speak to Sally about the trip, and I happened to hear your conversation. You are not going, Nicola, and that's final.'

'You wouldn't force me to stay behind?'

'It will be too much for your ankle. Am I right, Sally?'

'I think it might be,' Sally said unhappily.

'You can't do this to me, Jason!' Nicola protested. 'I've been looking forward to the trip.'

'You've also been looking forward to seeing the bridge,' he said, his voice cool and impersonal. 'If you do too much and strain your foot, you might not make it to the bridge. Would you consider the sacrifice worthwhile?'

There could be only one answer to that question.

Lance was upset when he heard that Nicola was not joining the expedition. Like her, he had been certain that the ankle would be up to the trip.

'I'll stay with you,' he said.

'Thanks, Lance, but it isn't necessary.'

'You can't remain here alone.'

'She won't be alone,' said Jason, coming up behind them. 'I'll be here.'

Nicola jerked. Stunned, she looked at Jason to see if he was serious. There was something rather terrifying about the thought of spending two days alone with him, for he had not spoken a pleasant word to her since her fall.

'You'll be here?' Lance looked equally stunned. 'But, Jason, you've always gone on the overnight expedition!'

'Which is why I don't need to go this time. I've seen it all many times. Besides, I have quite a bit of paperwork to catch up on.'

'Yes, but still. . .' Lance looked unhappy. 'I'll stay behind too.'

'I want you on that trip, Lance,' Jason said firmly.

'Nicola needs help.'

'Maybe she does, but remember that your first obligation is to the people on this tour. You have more experience than anyone else in the group. Remember too that Nicola's accident—while I'm sorry it happened—was entirely of her own making.'

Nicola tightened with anger. She saw the flush in

Lance's cheeks. 'Nicola's well-being concerns me,' he said tensely.

'There's no need for you to concern yourself. I'll make sure that she comes to no harm.'

'But, Jason——'

'I want you to start thinking about the trip, Lance.'

The ring of authority in Jason's voice was unmistakable. A man would have had to be a fool not to think twice about arguing with him when he was in this mood. Lance was no fool. Silently, unhappily, he dropped the issue and did not return to it.

The group left amid a great flurry of excitement. Linda said Nicola should not worry about meals—she would see to it that nobody was hungry. Sally hugged her, and said she would have stayed behind herself, but the expedition could not proceed without a nurse. As for Lance, with a defiant glance at Jason, he put his arm around Nicola and kissed her on the lips.

Minutes later they were gone. Nicola and Jason stood on the slope beyond the camp and watched them ride, single file, along the trail. Lance, as the leader, rode at the head of the group. The sun caught his red hair, so that even from a distance he was more visible than any of the others.

When the last of the horses was out of sight Nicola and Jason walked back down the slope. All morning there had been noise and laughter and excitement at the campsite. Now it was quite silent.

Nicola felt suddenly nervous. 'Thank goodness for Linda,' she said.

'Thank goodness indeed.'

They were speaking quietly, yet so intense was the silence all around them that their words echoed slightly.

'I like her very much. She's become a real friend.'

'I'm impressed with her too,' Jason said. 'Besides being a very nice person, she has a highly developed sense of responsibility.'

Nicola looked at him. 'Meaning I haven't?'

'Meaning that if Linda ever wanted a job with Adventure Tours, there'd be no test for her to pass first.' His eyes gleamed.

Nicola's anger flared to life in an instant. 'I should have known you'd find a way of getting back at me! You've never forgiven me for going up to the quarry and spraining my ankle.'

'You know very well that my anger has nothing at all to do with your ankle,' he said quietly.

'I do know. And I still say I did nothing wrong. I didn't mean to mislead you, Jason, but it's a waste of time telling you that, because you'll never believe me.'

He said nothing. He just stood there looking down at her. The gleam was still in his eyes. His lips tilted fractionally at the corners, but his jaw looked long and strong and somehow unyielding.

'Another thing,' Nicola said bitterly. 'Did you have to be so rough on Lance yesterday?'

'Was I rough?'

'You know you were. You said some awful things!'

'He was beginning to try my patience,' shrugged Jason.

'He was only being considerate. Lance wanted to stay behind because he thought that I needed him.'

'In the light of that parting kiss I witnessed,' Jason drawled, 'perhaps you needed him more than I realised.'

'There's nothing between Lance and me,' Nicola said flatly. 'There never has been. If you think I've encouraged him, then you're wrong.'

'But you'd have liked him to stay with you here nevertheless?'

She looked at him defiantly. 'Maybe I would. Lance is kind and gentle and he doesn't taunt me every chance he gets. At this moment I have no idea how we'll manage to get through two days alone together, Jason.'

'Seems to me we're already off to quite a start,' he said, without expression. 'The group hasn't been gone half an hour and already we're bickering.'

'That can end right now. You said you had work to do. I have too. It shouldn't be impossible for us to keep out of each other's way.'

That said, Nicola went to fetch her sketch-pad and the book where she had written up her notes from the different hikes. Emerging from her tent, she found that Jason was already bent over his papers. He did not ask her whether she wanted to sit with him, nor did he offer to get her a chair. He did not even look up. Taking a camp-stool, Nicola placed it in a sunny spot, as far from Jason as she could.

It was her intention to correlate her notes with her sketches, so that when her photographs were developed Todd would have comprehensive units of work to aid him in his research. She began to refine a sketch which she had done very roughly, only to find that the work was more difficult than she had imagined it would be. Perhaps because she was finding it so hard to concentrate.

Now and then, and always against her will, her eyes were drawn to Jason. In a figure-hugging T-shirt and shorts, he was so strong, so vital, that Nicola felt the familiar tightening in her stomach every time she looked at him. It was no good telling herself that he could be a hard and cruel man and that she was far better off without him. There was a part of her that never stopped yearning for him.

Once he looked up. Grey eyes clashed with brown

ones as he held her gaze for what seemed an interminable moment. In a second she was trembling, but she sat very still and hoped he would not notice. Then, coolly, deliberately, she bent her head and pretended to be engrossed in her work.

The sun rose in the sky. It grew hotter. On the trail, the group would have stopped to discard their sweaters and the sweat-pants they wore over their shorts. Glancing at her watch, Nicola knew it was noon and time for lunch.

Fleetingly she thought of asking Jason what he fancied, but decided against it. Going to the kitchen tent, she prepared a plate of sandwiches, cut up some fruit, and opened a beer. She put the lot on a tray which she carried outside to Jason.

'Lunch.' She motioned to him to put the tray on his lap.

'Looks good, Nicola, thank you. But this isn't all for me, surely? Aren't we going to share it?'

'I'm not hungry right now.'

'I see,' he said. There was a gleam in the eyes that touched her face, and she knew he did not believe her.

After he had eaten, Jason went off for a walk. Nicola tried hard not to watch the tall, broad-shouldered figure with the easy loping walk. She did not succeed. However, when he came back into view—she heard him whistling before she saw him—she made sure that all he saw of her was a head bent over a sketch-pad.

The sun was just beginning to set when she saw Jason light a fire.

She got to her feet and went over to him. 'I was about to ask you what you wanted for supper,' she told him.

He grinned at her. 'My treat this time.'

'What do you mean?'

'I'm making our supper tonight.'

'Cook only for yourself, Jason,' said Nicola.

His eyebrows rose. 'Really? You haven't eaten all day.'

'I'll make something when I feel like it.'

'What you're really trying to say is that you don't want to eat with me, Nicola.'

'We agreed to keep out of each other's way,' she said, more unsteadily than she would have wished.

'You said it. I don't remember agreeing.'

Taking a step towards her, he put his hands on her arms. The movement took her by surprise. In a moment she was quivering.

'It's. . .it's the only way,' she whispered.

'Nonsense! Let's call a truce, Nicola. At least let's have our meals together.'

'On one condition,' she said.

'What's that?'

'If it's a truce, then do you agree not to bring up the quarry? Or what you perceive as my other misdemeanours?'

'Agreed,' he said, with the smile that reached into her heart every time she saw it.

She sat by the fire and watched while he cooked them each a piece of steak and a *mielie*. When their dinner was ready, they took their plates and their chairs to a spot where they could watch the last of the sun setting over the high peaks in a wash of scarlet and golden colour.

It grew cool quickly after that. Nicola would have gone to her tent, but Jason persuaded her to keep him company a while longer. He put a log on the fire and they watched the flames spring to life.

For a while they sat in silence, so close together that they could have reached out and touched each other had they wanted to—and Nicola did want to. When they began to talk at last, it was without animosity. For the first time since that awful night when Jason had found out that she was Todd's sister, they talked of books and music and outdoor sports, of movies they had both seen. Nicola told Jason a bit about her work, and he told her of his dreams for expanding his company into other fields.

The sky had clouded over by the time they let the fire burn out and stood up and folded their camp-chairs. In the air was the sweet smell of impending rain.

At the entrance to Nicola's tent, Jason said, 'Thanks for a lovely evening.'

'It *was* a nice evening,' she agreed.

'I'm glad we have a truce, Nicola.'

'I'm glad too,' she said softly.

'I meant to ask you—does it scare you to be alone in the tent?'

'No, of course not.'

'Well, look, in case you need me—I've moved my things into the tent next to yours.'

She was a little surprised, but she only said, 'Thank you. I'm sure I won't need you.'

'Remember,' he said, 'you've only to call if you do.'

The noise was ear-shattering. A thousand canons booming. Lightning flashing somewhere close to the tent. Thunder crashing not a second later, again and again and again.

Nicola jerked up in fright as the thunder echoed and bounced from mountain to mountain. She had never heard anything like it. This was no ordinary thunderstorm. It was an orchestration straight out of hell.

Trembling, she lay back and huddled into her sleeping-bag with her eyes tightly closed and her hands clasped over her ears in a vain attempt to shut out the worst of the storm.

She did not see the tent flap move, the figure come in

and squat down beside her sleeping-bag. Until she felt two hands touching hers, she did not even know she was not alone. The shock of the contact brought a tearing scream to her lips.

'Nicola. . . Nicola, it's me.'

Her eyes snapped open, and she stared at him wide-eyed in the darkness. 'Good heavens!' she whispered.

'I'm sorry, I didn't mean to frighten you. Sweetheart, are you all right?'

The endearment did not register.

'Oh, Jason!' She flung her arms around his neck and pulled herself against him. 'You're here! Don't leave me, Jason.'

'I wouldn't think of leaving you,' he said.

CHAPTER NINE

JASON sat beside Nicola, holding her trembling body in his arms. While he held her, he caressed her, her hair, her back, her cheeks. The crashing of the thunder was no longer quite so terrifying in Nicola's ears, and gradually the trembling began to subside.

'Jason, you're wet!' she said suddenly.

'It's raining, sweetheart.'

This time she did hear the word. For a few seconds she was utterly still. His arms were still around her, and the damply masculine smell of him was in her nostrils. In the intervals between lightning flashes it was so dark in the tent that she could not see him. But she could feel him, and the feeling was terribly exciting, kindling something primal and primitive deep inside her, so that she wished the lower part of her body were not encased in the sleeping-bag.

'You came to me through this awful storm,' she said softly.

'I had to.'

'It's pouring! As for the lightning—you could have been struck.'

'I thought you might need me.'

'I did need you. I still need you very much.'

'Nicola. . .' he said in a husky tone she had never heard before, and she felt his lips move in her hair.

'I was petrified.' Her voice shook.

'I know.'

'I've never heard anything like it.'

'It's the mountains. The noise of the thunder is caught

150

between them. It bounces from one mountain to the other.'

'The echoes again,' she said.

'Yes, Nicola, our echoes.'

Our echoes. There was something very personal in the way he said the words.

'They're always changing, Jason. Like the ocean—storms change that too.'

'That's true. . .'

'You call out words, and it's just a game. And then something like this happens, and suddenly it's very frightening.'

'I never thought of it quite like that before. But you're right, of course.'

'It makes me realise that there's danger in the mountains.'

'There can be—sometimes,' Jason agreed.

'And that perhaps I was silly to go up to the quarry on my own.'

'Is this really my Nicola talking?' Against his cheek, she felt laughter bubbling in his throat.

'And yet I had to go, Jason. That hasn't changed. I suppose what I'm saying is a bit of a contradiction.'

'Like you, Nicola. You're a contradiction too.'

'What do you mean?' she asked.

With his arms still around her, he shifted his body and hers, so that they were both lying down. Nicola felt his head next to hers on the pillow, and she wished there was no sleeping-bag between them.

'You're such a gutsy girl,' he said. 'So incredibly feisty. I've never met anyone like you.'

'Haven't you?'

'No, sweetheart. And yet you're scared of a thunderstorm.'

'This is no ordinary storm,' she protested.

'I admit it, ordinary it isn't.'

'I keep thinking of the others. What will happen to them out there on the mountainside?'

'They're not "out there", as you put it. They're spending the night in huts that we erected specially for this expedition.'

'Then they're in no danger?' she asked in relief.

'No. Just as you're in no real danger, Nicola. If there's lightning overhead it will strike the trees rather than the tent.'

She was caught by something in his voice. 'What are you trying to say?' she asked after a moment.

'That tonight you've shown me a vulnerable side of you. It made getting a bit damp worthwhile.'

There was nothing actually lover-like in what he said. Nothing to justify the intense happiness she was feeling. But there it was—some things didn't need justifying.

'Talking about damp,' she said, with a briskness she was far from feeling, 'you're more than that. You have to get out of those clothes.'

'Now you really are talking!' Jason's voice was soft, dangerous. 'Lying here with you, there's nothing I want more than to take off my clothes.'

She was learning that desire could spring to life with all the rapidity of a veld-fire. That it could be a kind of pain spreading through her body.

'I was talking of a *change* of clothes,' she explained.

'And that's not what I'm talking of at all.'

'Jason!'

'Besides, what exactly did you have in mind?'

'I could give you some pyjamas. You wouldn't be able to close the buttons of the jacket, of course. And the trousers would be a bit short. . .'

Jason's burst of laughter stopped her.

'They would do in the meantime,' she said tentatively.

'They wouldn't do at all,' he said. He was not laughing now. 'Not when you and I are together. You know that, Nicola, don't you?'

'Jason, please. . .'

'Are you going to let me take off my clothes and lie with you in your sleeping-bag?'

'I don't think that's a very good idea,' she said, over the hunger that grew by the second.

'It's a wonderful idea.'

'The sleeping-bag is too small for two,' she said weakly.

'We could open it up. We could put a rug on the canvas and lie on that, and put the sleeping-bag over us.'

'I don't know. . .'

'You mean you've run out of excuses.'

'No,' she said, 'because there still happens to be the only excuse that matters.'

'What's that?'

'We're enemies.'

'Are we?' he smiled.

'You're angry with me. You feel I've deliberately deceived you from the moment we met.'

'We agreed not to talk about that for a while.'

'It's there all the same. It never seems to change.'

'Maybe,' he said. 'But we do have a truce. Let's keep to it.'

A truce was not a peace. This particular truce would end when the group returned to camp. Was it worth letting herself be soft and vulnerable with Jason, letting him breach all her defences when he would only turn against her afterwards? No, said her mind. *Yes!* said her heart.

'Actually,' he said softly, 'I think you should undress me.'

Nicola's heart thudded so hard against her chest that

she was certain he must hear it. 'Why do you want that, Jason?'

'Because it's much nicer that way, sweetheart.'

Nerves tightening inside her, she began to do as he asked. It was quite dark in the tent, but she did not need any light to guide her. Her fingers were trembling as she opened his shirt and slipped it from his shoulders. But once the shirt was off she found herself hesitating.

'You're not a coward, are you? Not my Nicola,' he taunted her softly.

'No. . .'

'Then finish what you started.'

Her breathing quickened as she unbuckled his belt. She almost stopped after that, but she did not want to be called a coward twice. Bravely, she unzipped his trousers, pulled them down and let him step out of them. She was relieved to find that beneath them he wore a pair of briefs.

'I. . . Jason, there's something I have to tell you,' she said unsteadily.

'Yes, sweetheart?'

'I've never. . . With anyone. . . Jason, I'm a virgin.'

He cupped her head with his hands. 'You keep surprising me, Nicola.'

'Does that mean you're disappointed?'

'No, sweetheart, it does not. How *could* it? In any case, I don't think we should——' He stopped. She waited for him to continue the thought, but he didn't.

Instead, he said, 'My turn to undress you now.'

'Yes. . .' It was becoming hard to breathe.

He undressed her with a slowness that was at once excruciating and terribly seductive. She had never been undressed by a man before—it was an intimacy she had never permitted—but she knew instinctively that nobody could equal the excitement that Jason was kindling inside her.

At last she was naked. Very shy now, she was in a hurry to get beneath the sleeping-bag. Not a word passed between them as they spread the rug on the canvas and opened the sleeping-bag over the rug. When they had finished, Nicola held up one corner of the bag and made to crawl underneath it.

'Wait,' said Jason.

'Why?'

'I want to look at you first.'

The worst of the storm had passed, but sporadic sheet lightning still lit the tent. Seconds after Jason had spoken lightning flashed again. Its duration was short, but for Jason it was enough. Nicola saw his eyes moving over her, worshipping her.

'I always knew you were beautiful.' His voice shook. 'You're even more beautiful than I imagined.'

His arms went around her, and she felt him against her, every inch of that long, hard body against her own softness. And then he said, 'Come,' and they bent down together and went under the sleeping-bag.

For at least a minute they lay quietly together, and Nicola savoured the coolness of Jason's skin wherever it touched hers. Inside her, her hunger had reached fever point. Just when she thought she could not wait another moment, Jason turned to her.

He did not kiss her, as she thought he would. Instead he began to touch her. Now brushing, now stroking, his hands moved over her, exploring, exciting, caressing. It was as if he meant to acquaint himself with every inch of her body. Almost as if he was laying claim to her, Nicola thought wildly, as if no man would ever be allowed to touch her after this. And no man would. She knew quite surely that after Jason there could be nobody else for her—ever.

He was exciting her more every moment, raising her to heights she had never imagined existed. His hands went to her breasts, cupping them, caressing them. Her nipples hardened in his fingers, and her pulse became a crazy racing thing.

At first she lay still, letting him explore where he wished. But then her own desire to know him as well as he was getting to know her got the better of her, and she began to touch him too. Her fingers found the back of his neck, his hard shoulders. Her hands pressed themselves flat-palmed to his chest. She explored his back and the hard, curved bones of his hips.

She heard the quickening of Jason's breath, and she knew that her touch was arousing in him the same desire he had aroused in her, and the knowledge that she had the power to do this to him gave her a feeling of intense and heady pleasure. Suddenly she knew that she had been waiting all night for this to happen. Perhaps she'd been waiting all her life.

At last he began to kiss her. He'd kissed her before, but never quite like this. There was no lightness in him now. No lightness in Nicola either, as she opened her lips to him. They kissed each other deeply, over and over again. Nicola could not have said afterwards how long they kissed.

It was Jason who lifted his head at length. 'In case you're wondering,' he said, 'we won't make love. Not all the way. . .'

'You don't want me. . .' she sighed.

'I want you so much. I want you desperately.'

With the tips of her fingers she traced the lines of his beloved face, and wondered what he would say if she told him she had never wanted anything quite so much as she wanted him at this moment.

'Neither of us is prepared, Nicola. You're a virgin, and so you. . . And I. . . This isn't the time for it.'

'I suppose not,' she whispered, though it hurt her to say the words.

'The storm is just about over. Perhaps it would be best if I just want back to my tent.'

'No—please! Jason, stay.'

'It means lying here with you and holding you in my arms while we sleep. *If* we sleep. Because I'm a normal man, Nicola, and it's going to kill me to lie with you and not do more than we're doing now.'

'Do you think it's easy for me?' she whispered in a strangled voice.

Jason made a noise in his throat and pulled her against him and kissed her again, more passionately than he had ever kissed her before. And then he rolled a little away from her. He was still holding her, but she felt the stiffness in his arms and legs, and guessed that the control he exercised was so enormous that it was driving him almost to breaking-point.

It took a long while for their heightened breathing to subside. Much longer for them both to sleep. Nicola wished she could stay awake all night, savouring the clean masculine smell of him in her nostrils and the feel of his skin against her own. But eventually, in the early hours of the morning, she did fall asleep.

When she woke it was to the smell of coffee. Opening her eyes, she saw Jason kneeling beside her. He held out a mug to her with the steam curling above it in a thin spiral. He had a mug too, and for a few minutes they sipped in silence.

'Sleep well?' he asked at last.

'Perfectly.'

'You felt marvellous in my arms, Nicola.'

She smiled at him, wanting to tell him what utter bliss the night have been for her. But all she said was, 'I think I like this truce.'

'So do I, sweetheart. Listen, why don't you get dressed while I make us some breakfast?'

'I thought that was my job on this trip.'

'These two days are an interlude. No designated jobs for either of us.'

An interlude was all it was, Nicola reminded herself as she dressed. It would be nice to think it could last, yet she was realistic enough to know that things would change when the group returned. Wonderful as the night had been, Jason had said nothing to indicate that he had changed his mind about trusting her.

He had rustled up a breakfast of fried eggs and sausages and some rather charred-looking toast, and he'd heated more coffee. It all tasted quite delicious to Nicola. When they had finished eating they went for a walk.

The storm had left a debris of fallen leaves and broken branches. The ground was sodden, but Nicola and Jason were wearing rubber boots, so the dampness did not disturb them. Halfway up the slope they came upon a sorry-looking protea.

'Good thing Lance pointed it out to me the first day, while it was still beautiful,' Nicola said.

'Yes, because it's a droopy thing today.' Jason paused in his step as he looked at her. 'All in all, Lance has shown you quite a bit, hasn't he?'

'He has. That's why I feel rather bad that I don't. . .' She stopped.

'Like him particularly?'

'How did you know?' she gasped.

'Am I right?'

'I do like him, Jason, but not in the way that he. . . Darn it, why is everything so complicated?'

'Is it?' He was laughing at her.

'Yes,' she said a little crossly. 'One thing I have to say about Lance, he couldn't have been kinder or more helpful. Todd will be amazed when he sees my photos. Now it just remains for me to find the purple aloe.'

'Which you're so sure that you'll find.'

She looked at him, her eyes sparkling with determination. 'If it's there I'll find it, Jason. I just have to hope that the storm didn't get to it.'

'Yes. . .' he said slowly.

'I also have to find Herman Tyler.'

'Don't get your hopes up too high, Nicola,' Jason warned.

'Lance said almost the same words,' Nicola told him.

'Did he really?'

'Yes, he did. But I *will* find Herman Tyler, and talk to him. And I'll prove both you and Lance—and anyone else who doesn't believe me—a bunch of cynics.'

They did not walk much further. It was still a bit strenuous for Nicola's recovering ankle, and the stony path was slippery after the rain. They spent the rest of the morning in camp, talking, laughing, just getting on together. Sometimes they were silent. But today it was the intimate silence of good friends rather than polite strangers.

It was almost noon when they heard the clopping of distant hoofs, and half an hour later the horses and their riders came into sight.

The group was almost back in camp when Nicola braved herself to ask Jason the question that had been on her mind all morning.

'Does this mean the end of our truce?'

'Do you want it to end?'

'No, of course not.'

'Then I don't see why it should,' Jason said, and she saw that his eyes were sparkling.

At last it was time to move on to the last camp, the one by the bridge. More precisely, about half a mile from the bridge, Nicola discovered, when they got there very late in the afternoon.

Their stay in this spot was going to be very short, just two nights and one day. After which it would be time to start the long downward trek back to the base camp.

'Maybe we could take a walk up to the bridge now?' Nicola said to Lance, who had barely left her side since he had returned from the expedition.

'You don't know what you're saying!' He looked horrified at the suggestion. 'It will be dark soon and the path is treacherous.'

'It's just that I'm so excited. I can't wait to see it!'

'I warn you—don't try going up there alone.'

'I learned that lesson when I went to the quarry.' She smiled at him. 'Don't look so anxious, Lance. I won't go traipsing up to the bridge in the dark. I've come this far, I suppose I can wait until tomorrow.'

Almost everyone stayed up late that night. They sat around the fire long after they had eaten. Jason brought out a few bottles of wine, but Nicola, who knew better than to mix wine with the mountain air, did not touch it. She made pot upon pot of coffee for all who wanted it.

When everyone was busy talking about tomorrow's last day on the tour, Linda drew Nicola aside.

'I've got something to tell you!' Her voice was alive with happiness.'

'Graham?' Nicola guessed.

'Yes! We've been getting on so well, Nicola, you know

that. And then the overnight trip—it was marvellous! We had so much fun together. I've never known anyone like Graham. And it turns out he feels the same way about me. Do you know, I even plucked up the courage to tell him about falling off the horse.'

'What did he say?'

'That he'd give me some riding lessons after we get back from the tour.'

'I get the feeling you're engaged,' Nicola smiled.

'We are—unofficially. We want to tell our families before we make it public. But I wanted you to know.'

'That's wonderful news!' Nicola gave her friend a warm hug. 'I'm so happy for you, Linda! I hope Graham knows how lucky he is to find you.'

It was close to midnight when they all went to their tents. Nicola was so tired that she just managed to take off her shoes before she flopped down on her sleeping-bag.

'Hey!' said Sally. 'Aren't you going to get undressed?'

'I don't have the energy,' Nicola muttered. 'I don't know why, but I'm exhausted.'

'Oh, really?' Sally was laughing. 'Come on, Nicola, open your eyes and get undressed. You can't go to sleep like that.'

'Leave me. . .'

But Sally, who had a strong sense of the correct order of things, did not let her be. 'Here,' she said, 'I'll help you. Poor thing, you really are pooped tonight, aren't you.'

When Nicola woke up she sensed, even though her eyes were closed, that the sun was already quite high in the sky. But her eyelids felt heavy, and her head was dull and heavy too.

The bridge! Suddenly she remembered where she was,

and what this special day would bring. She blinked twice, hard, forced her eyes open, and saw Sally sitting by her sleeping-bag watching her.

'What time is it, Sal? Lord, I feel awful!'

'Do you?'

'Yes, I don't know why. I meant to be up before dawn to make breakfast, but it looks as if I overslept.'

'You did,' said Sally.

'Oh, no! Does that mean I'll be in the dog-box again? And just when I was starting to get on better with Jason.'

'Nicola——'

'I'll have to get dressed quickly. Today's the day, Sally. I'm off to the bridge!'

Sally tried again. 'Nicola——'

'My head. . .' Nicola tried to sit up, and fell back. 'My head feels so heavy, Sally.'

'Does it?'

'Whatever it is, I have to shake it off.'

'Right,' Sally agreed.

'Have to get going. Just hold thumbs that I'll find what I'm looking for, Sal. The purple aloe and Herman Tyler.'

'Look, Nicola——'

'I have to hurry.' For the first time Nicola took in the tension in her friend's face, and realised that she'd kept interrupting her. 'Sally, what is it? What's happened?'

'The hike is over,' Sally told her.

'You don't know what you're saying. We're leaving straight after breakfast. Which I'd better see to in the next few minutes.'

'Nicola. . . I hate having to tell you this, but we had breakfast hours ago. Everyone's been to the bridge. They're already back. The sun is beginning to set, and it's almost time for supper.'

'That's impossible!' Nicola felt the blood draining from her cheeks as she jerked upright.

'It's true. I'm sorry, I'm so terribly sorry. I know how much this meant to you.'

'Why didn't you wake me?'

'I tried. We all tried.'

'*We?*' queried Nicola.

'Linda came to see what was happening. Jason was here. Even Lance. . .'

'I don't understand, Sally!'

'I'm not sure I do either. All I know is, there was no waking you, however hard we tried. We were getting quite worried about you.'

'That doesn't make sense!'

'You were very tired last night, exhausted. I had to undress you.'

'I think I remember. . .'

Sally hesitated a moment. Then she said, 'You must have had too much wine again.'

'That's not possible. All I had was coffee.'

'Lance seemed to think it was another hangover. And though I hate to admit it, he could have been right.'

'Don't you understand?' Nicola insisted. '*I didn't have any wine!*'

'Are you sure?' Sally looked a little shaken.

'Not a drop. I wouldn't have made that mistake again.'

'Then I don't understand. You slept as heavily as if you'd been drugged.'

Nicola stared at her friend. 'Say that again.'

'The way you slept. . . Just like a person who'd been drugged.'

'That's it!' Nicola exclaimed.

'What are you talking about?'

'*I was drugged!*'

'That's ridiculous!' protested Sally.

'No, it's not. I know for a fact that I had nothing to drink—not a drop. All I had last night was coffee. So it's the only explanation.'

'But who on earth would want to drug you?' Sally looked bewildered.

'The person who doesn't want me to go to the bridge.'

'Everyone wants to see you go there.'

'One person doesn't. I've made no secret of the fact that I want to clear Todd's name. Someone on this tour doesn't want me to find out what happened at the bridge that day.'

'Good grief!' Sally exclaimed. 'That's quite a thought!'

'I know I'm right—I *know* I am!' Nicola persisted.

'Do you have any idea who it could be?'

'No. . . All I know is that every member of staff was on the last tour as well. Which means it could be anyone.'

'I can promise you it wasn't me,' said Sally.

'Anyone except you,' Nicola said.

For a minute or two there was silence in the tent. Nicola sat with her head in her hands. She felt ill. At the same time she also felt an anger that grew by the second.

'What are you going to do?' Sally asked.

Nicola lifted her head. She looked at her friend with bleak eyes. 'I don't know. I do know that I have to do something. I will not let myself be defeated at this stage.'

A few curious glances were directed at Nicola as she arrived at the cooking fires. There were fewer enquiries as to whether she was feeling better. And no wonder! Nicola the lush, that must be how they thought of her. So be it, she decided grimly, she would say nothing to disillusion them. Not tonight, anyway. If they wanted to think she'd been suffering the effects of too much wine, let them. She would wait until she had evidence of

Todd's innocence before she said a word in her own defence.

Suddenly Lance was at her side. 'Nicola—you're up! I was getting awfully concerned about you. Are you all right?'

'I'm fine,' she assured him.

'You don't know how terrible I felt, going to the bridge without you. We did try to wake you——'

'I know. Sally told me.'

'It's such a terrible shame that we have to leave tomorrow morning, but the schedule is all set. It seems we can't delay the return back.'

'I know,' she said.

'Todd will be upset.'

'He'll get over it. He never really thought I'd get as far as I did anyway.'

'You seem to be taking this set-back extraordinarily well.' He looked surprised.

'Because it's over now, isn't it? There's no point moping about it. At least Todd will have all the photos I managed to take.'

Turning away from Lance, Nicola saw that Linda had already put out the meat on a big wooden board together with a pile of parboiled potatoes in their jackets. Nicola laid the meat on the grid, and within seconds the mouth-watering smell of barbecuing meat filled the air. It was a smell she would forever associate with the tour. Though after today with no pleasure.

She turned away from the fire, and looked upwards into the cleft. Somewhere up there was the bridge. As well as the answer to a secret. She had spoken brave words to Sally, but inside her there was a growing feeling of uncertainty. Was there any chance at all that she could still learn the truth?

She started when Jason said, 'Nicola. . .' The sizzling of the meat had shut out his footsteps.

'I've just come from your tent,' he said. 'Sally said you were awake and that you were feeling all right.'

'I'm fine. Great,' she assured him.

'Are you sure? No headache? No pain or nausea?'

'I'm fine, really. Listen, Jason, I'm sorry about the supper. I'd planned a special meal for tonight, but in the end there was no time to make it.'

He stood looking down at her a moment, his eyes hooded and unreadable. Then he gestured to her to take a few steps with him, away from anyone who might be listening.

'What happened?' he asked.

'I slept. Seventeen hours of uninterrupted beauty sleep.'

'Why?'

She shrugged. 'I must have been tired.'

'Stop it, Nicola! This silly flippancy doesn't suit you.'

'I'm sorry, but I don't know what else to say,' she explained. 'I've had one hangover—remember? This must have been more of the same.'

'Is that what you think?'

She looked up at him, at the lean, chiselled face with the high cheekbones; at the sensuous lips that had taken her to heights she had never dreamed existed; at the eyes she loved so much. Even now she loved him. And she wished with all her heart that at least with Jason she could be open. But Jason was as much under suspicion as anyone else.

'I'm not sure what to think,' she said lightly. 'I remember very little about last night. I'm sorry, Jason, I can't tell you more than that.'

'I see,' he said. And then, 'How do you feel about not getting to the bridge?'

'Disappointed,' she admitted.

'Upset?'

'Yes,' she said, looking at him directly, 'I do feel extremely upset. But since we're turning back tomorrow I have to find a way of coming to terms with my feelings, don't I?'

The *braaivleis* had ended. So had the sing-song. Nicola reached the tent first. A few minutes later Sally arrived. She stopped short when she saw Nicola with a heavy jacket over her sweater and a torch in her hand.

'Going somewhere?' she asked.

'For a walk.'

'*Now*? It's late.'

'I'm going to the bridge,' Nicola told her.

Sally stifled a gasp. 'You can't do that!'

'I have to. You know we're leaving tomorrow morning. If I don't go tonight it will be too late.'

'You're crazy! You can't do this, Nicola.'

'I have to,' Nicola insisted.

'Anything could happen to you.'

'I have to risk it. Obviously, I'll never find the purple aloe. But I do have to see Herman Tyler.'

'You can't go alone. Get one of the men to go with you.'

'*No*! Don't you see? I don't want anyone trying to stop me again.'

'You don't even know the way,' protested Sally.

'There's only one trail, and I think I know the general direction. I have the torch, and I can shine it as soon as I get beyond the camp. I'll find the way.'

'I don't like what you're doing, Nicola,' said Sally worriedly.

'Do you think I like it? Listen, Sal, apart from you not another soul must know about this. I really wish you

didn't have to know either—I hate having to involve you
at all—but if I didn't tell you, you'd wonder where I
was, and you'd raise the alarm.'

'Let me tell Craig.'

'No!' said Nicola firmly.

'I know he didn't drug you.'

'I don't think he did either, but I can't take the risk.'

'At least tell Jason,' Sally pleaded.

'I can't,' Nicola said through the pain that had been
in her heart all that evening. 'I can't tell anyone because
I don't know who drugged me.'

'Then I'll come with you myself.'

'You're a good friend.' Nicola gave her a hug. 'But
I've involved you enough as it is. I have to do this alone,
Sally.'

She knew where the trail began, for she had made a
point of looking for it while it was still light enough to
see. It had looked harmless enough then: a narrow path
meandering away through the scrub. In the dark, it was
a different proposition altogether.

Nicola hesitated as she left the reassuring confines of
the campsite and stood at the head of the trail. Suddenly
she was very nervous. With only the ephemeral light of
the stars and a thin crescent moon to guide her, at least
until she was far enough from camp to use her torch,
this walk was going to be a lot more difficult—and
frightening—than the hike up to the quarry had been.

She began to walk. Deliberately, carefully, she put
one foot in front of the other. Very faintly she could
make out the direction of the trail. A yard or two further
on and it would start to curve. Not long after that she
would be out of sight of the camp and could use the
torch.

The curve was upon her when a stone skittered

somewhere beyond her. Abruptly she stopped. Nothing moved. Perhaps a *dassie* or a fieldmouse scampering through the scrub had loosened a pebble. The sound might even have been nothing more than a product of her imagination. She began to walk again.

A tall, dark shape moved suddenly on to the path. It came towards her. Nicola's heart skipped a few beats and her skin went cold.

She screamed. At the same time a voice she knew said, 'Nicola!'

CHAPTER TEN

NICOLA would have screamed again, but Jason clamped a hand over her mouth.

'Quiet, Nicola. . .'

'Let me go!' She tried to shout the panicked words against the palm of his hand.

His hand left her mouth and she said furiously, 'Don't ever do that again!'

'I'm sorry I scared you—I didn't mean to. But I couldn't let you scream again.'

'You didn't want anyone to hear me. . .'

'That's right.' His arms went around her. 'You're shaking, Nicola.'

'What do you expect after the fright you gave me?' she demanded.

'Are you all right?'

'I will be in a moment. What are you doing here, Jason?'

'I was waiting for you.'

She was more frightened than ever now. 'Why would you be doing that?'

'I knew it was only a matter of time before you'd come this way.'

'You couldn't have known. . .'

'I did.'

Nicola looked up at him, trying in vain to read his expression in the dark. 'Sally told you?' she asked at last, disbelievingly.

'Nobody told me anything.'

'Then how. . .? I mean, why would you think. . .?'

'I happen to know my Nicola. I know that she's not only single-minded and stubborn, she's also the bravest girl I ever met.'

The way he said it might have made her feel happy, but the day's events had put her on her guard.

'Actually,' she said brightly, 'I'm just out for a walk.'

'A walk up to Herman's hut.'

The muscles in her stomach contracted. 'I'm going alone,' she said after a moment, understanding that there was no point in trying to keep up the bluff.

'No, Nicola, you are not!'

'Don't try to stop me!' she warned.

'I won't stop you. I know this is something you feel you have to do.'

'It is,' Nicola assured him.

'But I'm going with you.'

'*No!*'

'There's no point in arguing the matter. It's quite later as it is.'

She took a step away from him. 'You don't understand. . .'

'I understand that I won't let you take another foot along this path unaccompanied.'

'Jason, was it you. . .?' Her voice shook. She stopped, unable to say the words.

'No, sweetheart, I didn't drug you.'

She gasped. 'You *knew* I was drugged?'

'Of course.'

'Oh, lord!' She took another step away from him.

'I didn't do it.' His voice reached out to her. 'You'll just have to believe me.'

'Who did?'

Jason was silent a moment. Then he said, 'I'm hoping we'll find out.'

'We. . .?' she queried.

'Do you still not understand that I'm coming with you? I'd be crazy if I let you go alone. Look, Nicola, I know how you feel. You think there's nobody you can trust.'

'Right. . .'

'But you have to trust somebody. Don't you think it could be me?'

She *did* trust him. She knew that suddenly. Even if it made no sense at all, she trusted him.

'All right,' she said.

They began to walk, and she found that she was glad when he took her hand. The feel of the strong fingers entwined with hers made her feel safe.

'You hand is damp,' he said.

'Sheer fright,' Nicola admitted.

'And yet you were prepared to go on all the same. Didn't it ever occur to you that what you were doing was foolhardy?'

'Actually,' she admitted, 'I came very close to turning back. But I made Todd a promise. I couldn't let a bit of nervousness get in the way.'

'My gutsy girl,' said Jason, and laughed softly.

As soon as he was certain that they were out of sight of the camp, Jason shone his torch. With the slender beam lighting up the trail, the last of Nicola's nervousness vanished.

'I never dreamed it would be quite so far,' she said, when they'd been walking about half an hour.

'In the mountains any distance takes time,' Jason told her. 'But we're almost there now.'

She was surprised to see him peering intently at the ground as they walked. Every few yards they paused as he shone the torch ahead and a little to the right.

The beam stopped suddenly on a small, pyramid-shaped pile of stones. 'This way,' said Jason, and led Nicola off the trail and into the scrub.

'You're sure this is right?' she asked doubtfully.

'Quite sure.'

'Where's the bridge?'

'A little further along the trail. But Herman's shack is back here, hidden in the bush.'

'I would have come all this way on my own, and I'd never have found it. . .' She was trembling again.

'If I hadn't put up the stones as a marker, I wouldn't have found it in the dark either,' Jason told her.

'*You* put them here?'

'That's right.'

'When?'

'This morning.'

'You're not saying. . .? Jason, did you go to Herman's shack?'

'Yes.'

'*Why?*'

'You were so sure that he knew something. I had to give it a try.'

'What did he say?' Nicola demanded urgently.

'I didn't see him, he wasn't there. But there were signs that the shack was inhabited, which makes me think he'll be there now.'

'All of a sudden I feel very nervous,' she said. 'What if he doesn't know anything after all? If we've come all this way for nothing?'

'Even if he does know something, he might not want to tell us. You'd better prepare yourself for that, Nicola. I've seen Herman around in the past. He's a bit of a grouch, and he doesn't like the tour group.'

'He *must* tell us. . .'

'Look,' said Jason, and waved the torch. 'There it is.'

From the little Nicola could see, the shack was small and a bit ramshackle. On one side of it were a few water barrels and a cart. From somewhere behind the shack came the sound of neighing and the stomping of hoofs.

'Horses.' Nicola was whispering now. 'I wondered how he managed to cope up here. Food, things like that.'

'He's a resourceful type. Somehow he manages. I believe the quarry is a useful base of sorts when he needs it.'

They were almost at the shack now. A dim light shone behind dusty window-panes.

At the door they stopped and glanced at each other. Then Jason knocked. There was no response and he knocked again. Nicola bit down hard on her lower lip to hide her trembling.

Creaking, the door opened a few inches. A rough voice called, 'Yeah?'

'My Tyler?' said Jason.

'Yeah.'

'My friend and I would like to talk to you.'

A few seconds passed. Then the door opened wider. A lamp swung over their faces.

'Talk,' the man invited.

'Can we come inside, Mr Tyler?'

A few seconds more. Then the door opened just far enough to let Jason and Nicola step into the shack.

Small and wiry, with stubble covering much of his face and a beard that reached to the middle of his chest, Herman Tyler looked as tough a man as Nicola had ever seen. His overalls looked as if he'd worn them all his life, and the soles of his *veldskoene* were attached with twine to the upper parts of his shoes.

'You're from the camp,' he said aggressively.

'Yes,' Jason said.

'Suppose you're lost.'

'No. We came here to talk to you. But first'—Jason

took two small brown paper bags from his pockets—
'these are for you.'

'What's this?' demanded Herman Tyler suspiciously.

'Tobacco and sugar. Thought you might have some
use for them.'

'Don't need no charity.'

'We know that, Mr Tyler. And it isn't charity, it's a
gift. I know you haven't always had good feelings for our
tour group.'

'Bloody nuisance—people traisping all over the place.
A man can't be quiet, can't think with all those folk
around.'

'I know, and I'm sorry, I really am,' Jason apologised.
'We don't mean to disturb you. That's why we brought
you these things. An offering of friendship.'

'Don't need them—but I may as well take them.'

As Herman took the packets Jason had brought and
put them down on a table. Nicola looked around her.
Dilapidated the place might be, but it was also obvious
that the old man was comfortable. All around him were
the things that mattered to him: his prospecting tools
leaning against a wall; an old tea-chest with some cups
and plates and a few groceries on it; a bed and a couple
of chairs; and on one wall some yellowed newspaper
clippings and pictures which dated back to an era when
all the land had been a prospectors' haven.

'There's something we want to ask you,' Jason said,
when Herman turned back to them.

'Figured you had a reason for coming up here.'

'A few months ago there was an accident at the bridge.
A group was crossing over and the bridge collapsed. Do
you remember it?'

'Why wouldn't I?'

'The next day we found a sign warning that the bridge

was not safe to walk on. It was lying in the bushes. The group leader said he'd never seen it.'

Herman looked at them in silence.

'What we want to know,' Jason went on, 'is how the sign came to be in the bushes.'

'Fellow put it there,' said Herman.

'Which fellow? Do you remember?'

'Sure. Nothing wrong with my memory.'

'Can you describe him?'

'Tall man—angry look.'

'Anything else you can tell us about him?'

'Red hair.'

'*Lance*?' breathed Nicola after a hushed moment. Her eyes, shocked and a little dazed, met Jason's. 'It must have been Lance. . . There's nobody else with red hair.'

If Jason was as shocked as she was, his casual manner certainly did not betray it. 'A redheaded man, you say? Do you know when he hid the sign?'

'Arrived some time before the others. Took the sign out of the ground. Threw it behind a bush and went back down the trail.'

'I see.' Jason looked at Nicola again. Then he said to Herman, 'I suppose you didn't think of warning the rest of the group?'

The prospector shrugged. 'Why should I? Their problem, not mine. Wasn't up to me.'

'Someone could have been hurt.'

'Told you—that camp of yours is a darned nuisance. Shouldn't be up here in the first place,' grumbled Herman.

'How about the next day? A few of us came back to look around. . . Did you see us?'

'Don't stand around gawking, if that's what you mean. Got better things to do.'

'The redheaded man was with me,' Jason told him.

'I saw him,' Herman admitted.

'You didn't say anything then either.'

'Nobody asked me.'

It was as simple as that. Since nobody had asked Herman what had happened, he'd felt under no obligation to talk about what he knew. It was impossible to argue with his particular brand of logic, Nicola realised. Evidently Jason's thoughts were the same as her own, for her said, 'You've been very helpful, Mr Tyler. Thank you, we appreciate it very much.'

A few yards away from the shack, Nicola turned to Jason. 'Todd didn't do it! He *didn't do it!*'

His arms closed around her, and for a few moments they held each other tightly in the cool, sweet-smelling darkness. A minute passed. Then Jason peered down at her.

'Will you believe me when I say I'm as happy as you are?'

'Yes! Oh, yes! I always told you he didn't do it.'

'I know, sweetheart, and you were right. I only wish I'd had your faith in Todd.'

'He's my brother, and I love him. I knew he wouldn't stoop to doing such a dreadful thing.'

Jason cupped her face with his hands. 'Do you always have such total faith in the people you love?'

'Mostly. . .' she said unsteadily. She would have said 'always', but she remembered that there had been a time today when she'd felt there was nobody she could trust—not even Jason.

'It's the lucky person who's loved by you,' he said. He drew her to him again.

His kiss was deep and searching, and in a moment Nicola was responding with all the love and ardour that was in her. She would willingly have spent the night on the trail in Jason's arms.

As it was, he lifted his head and looked down at her. 'We have to get back.'

'Do we?' she asked provocatively. 'It seems we have to go back every time.'

'You're a witch, do you know?' Jason's laughter was a little ragged. 'I'd love to remain up here with you, but there's something I still have to do tonight.'

Nicola did not ask him what that was. It was not difficult to guess.

It was only when they were walking once more that she said, 'I'm not sure why, but I had a feeling you weren't surprised to hear about Lance.'

'I wasn't—not then.'

'You couldn't have known all along that he was responsible.'

'Obviously I didn't.' He sounded troubled. 'I blamed Todd for the accident, you know that. I regret it very much now—but at the time there seemed no other explanation.'

'I understand,' Nicola said generously.

'And then. . . I saw how deeply you believed in Todd's innocence. At first, I admit, I thought you were just prejudiced. But after a while I began to wonder— could you possibly be right? And if Todd didn't hide the sign, then who did?'

'You still haven't told me why you weren't surprised to hear it was Lance. Of all people! He's been so wonderful to me all along.'

'That's it,' Jason explained. '*Too* wonderful. It's never been Lance's way to get himself so attached to anyone. I became more and more puzzled by it. It's only in the last day or so that isolated things began to make sense.'

'Such as?'

'He was so eager to help you get pictures, for one thing. But many of the flowers he showed you were not all that unusual.'

'I didn't know——' Nicola began.

'Don't get me wrong, Nicola—Todd will be thrilled to have them. All I'm saying is that Lance showed too much enthusiasm when it wasn't warranted.'

'I had no idea,' she confessed.

'How could you? And then this morning, when I realised you'd been drugged——'

'You said that earlier. And it's true, Jason—I was drugged. But how did you know?'

'I was quite certain it wasn't a hangover—though Lance suggested it must be. You see, I'd been with you all evening and you'd had no wine. All you had was coffee.'

'That's right,' she agreed.

'And I remembered seeing Lance pouring you a cup.'

'You think he put something in the coffee?'

'It's likely, isn't it? I remembered the first time you'd slept so late. I accused you of having a hangover, but I realise now it wasn't that at all. He must have given you something then too.'

'*Yes*! I never did understand why a few glasses of wine would affect me like that.'

'I said some terrible things to you that morning, Nicola,' Jason murmured.

'I forgive you.' There was a smile in her voice. Then she said, 'I think I understand about last night—Lance wanted to make sure I wouldn't find Herman Tyler.'

'That's right,' he agreed.

'But what about the first time? What was he trying to accomplish then?'

'I've been thinking about that. I believe he wanted me to fire you. You were a danger to him, Nicola, don't you see? From the moment he realised you were Todd's sister he knew he had to find a way of getting rid of you.'

'Yes. . .'

'The afternoon you went to the quarry—it was more of the same. He realised how angry I'd be, and he couldn't wait to let me know what you'd got up to.'

'The strange thing is,' Nicola said slowly, 'that he was so possessive. . .so terribly jealous of you, Jason. We had a dreadful scene after I sat with you at the fire. He implied that what he wanted from me was more than friendship.'

'I believe it was only his way of diverting suspicion away from himself. You'd have found his interest in the waning very quickly once the tour was over. As for his jealousy—he must have thought it would be dangerous if you and I became too close. I might have been tempted to believe your defence of Todd. And he was right— that's what happened.'

They were almost back at the campsite when Nicola said, '*Why*? I still don't understand *why* he did it.'

'I have my thoughts on that too,' said Jason. 'I have to find out if I'm right.'

Sally burst into tears of relief when Nicola walked into the tent almost two hours after she had left it. Every minute had seemed like eternity for poor Sally who had been very tempted to go to Craig for help in finding Nicola.

After swearing her to secrecy until the rest of the group was officially told the truth, Nicola told her what she and Jason had discovered that night.

At first, Sally was astonished. But when she'd considered the news a few minutes, Nicola was surprised to see how quickly she accepted it.

'I'm so *glad* Todd's name has been cleared,' Sally kept saying.

'I can't wait to get back and tell him,' Nicola agreed.

'And now the way is clear for you and Jason as well.'

'I doubt it,' Nicola said slowly.

'I don't understand. . .'

'My own part in all this hasn't changed. As far as Jason is concerned, I conned myself on to the trip. I lied and deceived him. . . Don't you see, Sally? Todd's innocence and Jason's lack of trust in me are two different issues.'

'I don't believe it!'

'Jason has said absolutely nothing to make me think otherwise.'

Long after Sally was asleep, Nicola was still awake. Would Jason come to her after his talk with Lance? She lay in the dark, her ears straining for the sound of footsteps. All she heard was the shrilling of the crickets. Of Jason there was no sign.

The group came to life earlier than usual the next morning. With many hours of riding ahead of them, it was necessary to make an early start.

Nicola caught glimpses of Jason, but he was so busy talking to different members of staff and checking on the day's arrangements that she had no chance to speak to him.

She saw Lance as well. Dour-faced and ashen, he made an obvious point of avoiding her. Just as well, she decided grimly, for after all Lance had put Todd through she doubted that she would be able to say a word to him without losing her temper.

Andy and Sam had the pack-horses ready, and the riding horses were saddled. Soon after breakfast, tourists and staff took a last look round before getting ready for the first lap of their descent through the mountains.

Nicola was about to guide her horse down the slope when Jason came up alongside her.

'Stay behind,' he said quietly—the first words he had spoken to her since the previous night.

Her head jerked up, and there was a question in her eyes.

'Let the others go,' he said. 'We'll catch up with them later.'

'*Why?*' In a moment her pulses were racing.

'Because you and I have some unfinished business to attend to.' He smiled at her startled look, and she saw that his eyes were sparkling.

A few minutes later the riders were on the trail. Nicola and Jason watched them go—Sally beside Craig, Linda with Graham. In the lead, far ahead of everyone else, almost as if he could not wait to break his connection with the rest of the group now, was Lance. His red hair was faintly gilded by the first rays of the morning sun.

When the last of the riders had vanished from sight, Jason turned to Nicola. 'Let's go. We'll leave the horses here and pick them up later.'

'The bridge?' she asked.

'Where else?'

She looked at him, aware that her heart was in her eyes, knowing she could do nothing to conceal how she felt. 'I'd given up all hope of getting there,' she confessed.

He ran his fingers along the curve of her cheeks, then pushed a strand of hair gently from her forehead. 'I don't know if I can ever make full amends to Todd,' he said, 'but at least I can do something. Don't forget your camera, Nicola.'

'Do you think we'll find the purple aloe?' Her voice shook.

'If it's there.'

On their return from the bridge, Jason said, they would pick up the horses, and then they would ride down the trail. He had arranged with Craig that the group would wait for them at the first picnic spot.

The path that led to the bridge looked quite different in the morning light. Nothing sinister or dangerous about it now. It was just a narrow path winding away through the scrub.

They passed the little pyramid of stones, but this time they did not turn off. Jason took Nicola's hand as they went on along the trail.

'I know now why Lance did it,' he told her.

'You talked to him last night?'

'After I left you, yes. At first he denied everything. The very idea that he'd remove a warning sigh was defamatory as well as absurd.'

'Did you tell him about Herman Tyler?'

'Yes. He broke down quite quickly after that.'

'Why did he do it, Jason? I can't think of a single reason.'

'Good old-fashioned jealousy and competition. It seems that Lance and Todd were after the same botany lectureship at the university. Lance knew very well that he couldn't compete with Todd either personally or professionally. He'd seen how people were drawn to Todd on our tours, and he knew it would be the same with students. And then there was Todd's book. It could become an important textbook.'

'He didn't want Todd to get a picture of the purple aloe. Without it the book wouldn't be complete,' said Nicola.

'That's right.'

'But what was the point of hiding the sign? He knew Todd would never make it across the bridge anyway.'

'The purple aloe was just one part of the whole thing, Nicola,' Jason explained. 'Todd was the leader of the group, the others followed where he led. By making it look as if he would stop at nothing to get what he wanted—to the point of endangering people's safety—Lance knew Todd would be discredited.'

'I can't believe anyone would go to such lengths.' Nicola felt a little ill.

'Lance was desperate. He'd set his heart on the position. He *had* to have it. Besides being desperate, I realise now—too late, unfortunately—he's also a little deranged.'

'I shouldn't feel sorry for him,' warned Nicola.

'No.'

'And yet I do. To want something *that* badly. . . What will you do to him, Jason?'

'The damage to his career will be punishment enough, I think.'

She looked at him. 'What do you mean?'

'The moment we get back I'll contact the university and let them know the truth. All of it. I'll also contact the papers that reported the incident. I think you'll find that Todd's telephone will start ringing soon after that.'

'I don't know what to say. . .'

'Don't say anything,' he said gruffly. 'I wish Todd could have been spared all the unhappiness. The very least I can do now is put things right.'

They came to the bridge, a narrow bridge that swayed a little when they walked on it. Beneath it tumbled the stream in which Todd had lost his photos.

And then they were on the other side. They walked silently now, their eyes searching the arid ground on all sides.

They nearly missed it. If they had not been looking so intently they might never have spotted it at all. It was on a high cliff, almost lost behind a pile of loose stone.

Jason helped Nicola climb to it. Remembering the storm, and the debris it had caused, she was very nervous now. Would there be anything left of Todd's aloe to photograph?

It was only when they came to it that they saw the rock-face jutting out from the cliff. Not quite a cave, more like an awning.

'A natural shelter!' Nicola was astonished.

'The storm never got to it.' The relief in Jason's voice showed that his thoughts had been the same as Nicola's. 'And isn't a beauty?'

'What an exquisite colour!'

'Look at the shape. It's different from anything I've ever seen.'

'No wonder Todd was after it,' Nicola said.

In her camera was an unused film. She shot the aloe from every angle. By the time she had finished, there was not a picture left on the film.

At last she looked up at Jason—and saw that he had been watching her.

'Happy?' he asked.

'Elated! I had two purposes when I came on this tour, Jason, and I achieved them both. There were times when I didn't think I would achieve either of them.'

'I had a double purpose too, sweetheart.'

There was something in his tone that made the blood turn to fire in her veins. She looked at him, and then away. But he caught her face in his hands, in that way of his that was so seductive, and forced her to meet his eyes again.

'Don't you want to hear about it?' he asked softly.

'Yes. . .' she said unsteadily.

'I came on this tour, Nicola, because I wanted to get to know you better. I discovered that the girl who'd intrigued me in Cape Town was everything I'd thought she'd be—only more so. Beautiful and desirable and sexy. Kind and thoughtful. Independent and brave beyond anything I expected.'

'You also learned that you couldn't trust me.'

'*But I can.* I was wrong about that all the time.'

'What are you saying?' she whispered. 'You were so angry that I didn't tell you the truth about Todd, about the quarry.'

'I know, my darling. I was terribly angry. It took me a long while—far too long—to see that there was another side to what you did.'

'Jason. . .?' she queried.

'It was never dishonesty that drove you, Nicola. It was loyalty. A loyalty to your brother that was so important to you that there were certain things you had to do.'

'Yes!'

'That was never the case with Serena. With my ex-wife. . . There was more to it than that she couldn't accept my kind of life. She used my absences to have an affair with another man, and even when I started to get suspicious she kept denying it.'

'I didn't know that,' Nicola said quietly.

'Not many people do. It was her *disloyalty* to me that destroyed any feelings I had for her. I was bitter for a long time after we separated. I was determined never to be hurt again. Never to let anyone be close enough to hurt me again.'

Jason, tough, confident, independent Jason was vulnerable! Compassion welled up inside Nicola. If anything, it made her love him more.

'Anyone except you,' he said.

Her throat was dry, and her heart hammered so hard against her chest that she was sure he must hear it.

His hands had tightened on her face. His thumbs began a slow, drugging movement up her cheeks and down.

'My second purpose,' he said, his eyes never leaving hers, 'was to persuade you to be my wife.'

Nicola had never imagined it was possible to feel the degree of happiness that she was experiencing now. It filled her mind, her body, her bloodstream. It reached to the very core of her being.

'I love you so much,' he said, drawing her to him. 'You're part of me, Nicola. I can't lose you. I can't let you go!'

'You won't have to.' She gave him a look, part tremulous, part provocative.

'You mean you'll marry me?'

'Yes! Oh, yes! I love you too, my darling Jason. I've loved you all along.'

'I'll arrange things so that I won't have to travel. . .so that I won't have to be away from home,' he said. 'I have enough trained people who can lead the tours now.'

'But you love travelling.'

'I don't want to leave you.'

'I'll come with you, my darling. I enjoy this adventurous life of yours.'

He looked at her wonderingly. 'What about your career, Nicola?'

'I won't have to give it up, I'll do it part time. I've reached a stage where I can choose my assignments.'

'Have you any idea how much I love you?' he asked huskily.

'As much as I love you?'

'A hundred times as much! A thousand. I'm going to

spend the rest of my life making you happy, my darling Nicola.'

'I don't think I could be any happier than I am at this moment,' she said raggedly.

They sank on to the ground beside Todd's aloe, and began to kiss. Kisses of love and promise and commitment. Kisses that seemed to have no ending, because their love would never end.

After a while they remembered where they were, and that people were waiting for them, and they stood up. Arms tightly around each other, they began to walk back to the bridge.

MILLS & BOON

NEW AUTHORS

**ALL BRAND NEW SERIES
FEATURING BOTH ESTAB-
LISHED AND UP AND
COMING AUTHORS.**

**ROMANCE FICTION
FEATURING BELIEV-
ABLE CHARACTERS
AND PASSIONATE
EMOTIONS.**

4 FREE BOOKS!

ORDER NOW!

YES! Please send me FOUR FREE INTRODUCTORY MILLS & BOON titles
and at the same time enrol me as a subscriber to HARLEQUIN MILLS & BOON
BOOK CLUB. I understand that each month I will receive 4 BRAND NEW titles
at the special discount price of only $2.70* each (plus $1.15** postage and handling)
a total of $11.95***. I am under no obligation and may cancel at anytime but my
FOUR FREE books are mine to keep forever.

Name (Mrs/Miss/Ms) _____
PLEASE PRINT

Address _____

_____ State_____ Postcode_____

Signature _____
(If under 18, please have an adult sign for you.)

Publisher reserves the right to accept or reject orders. Terms and prices subject to change without
notice. Offer limited to one order per household and not valid to current Mills & Boon
subscribers.

SEND NO MONEY — MAIL TODAY!

To: Harlequin Mills & Boon
P.O. Box 810, Chatswood, N.S.W. 2067
(72-74 Gibbes Street, Chatswood, N.S.W. 2067)
or
New Zealand Readers
Private Bag, Henderson, Auckland 1231, New Zealand

*NZ price $3.50
**NZ price $1.95   Offer expires 15/11/90.
***NZ price $15.95 (incl. G.S.T.)   CBP89.

This offer not available outside Australia and New Zealand.

GREAT NEWS!!

Mills & Boon *introduce*
Four new titles each month featuring up
and coming as well as established authors

Titles available next month —

RUNNING SCARED by Jenny Arden
SECRET WHISPERS by Anne Beaumont
THE DEVIL'S FLOWER by Jane Donnelly
NO REGRETS by Kathryn Ross

DON'T MISS THEM

$3.25*

(Aust. Recommended Retail)
*New Zealand $4.50 (Inc. G.S.T.)

Look out for these two great Medical Romances this month

Read more about the lives and loves of doctors and nurses in the fascinatingly different backgrounds of contemporary medicine. These are the two Doctor Nurse romances to look out for this month.

REPENTANT ANGEL
by Lynne Collins

A MEDICAL LIAISON
by Sharon Wirdnam